BREATHLESS
A STORY OF DOMINANCE
AND SUBMISSION

Jenika Snow

LOVEXTREME

Siren Publishing, Inc.
www.SirenPublishing.com

A SIREN PUBLISHING BOOK
IMPRINT: LoveXtreme

BREATHLESS: A STORY OF DOMINANCE AND SUBMISSION
Copyright © 2012 by Jenika Snow

ISBN-10: 1-61926-930-9
ISBN-13: 978-1-61926-930-9

First Printing: April 2012

Cover design by Jinger Heaston
All cover art and logo copyright © 2012 by Siren Publishing, Inc.

PUBLISHER
Siren Publishing, Inc.
www.SirenPublishing.com

DEDICATION

I promise not to let go if you promise not to fade away. It's the times when you leave me breathless that matter the most.

BREATHLESS: A STORY OF DOMINANCE AND SUBMISSION

JENIKA SNOW

Chapter One

"I'm not a prostitute." Lalita couldn't believe she was actually contemplating calling the number on the card she held. "You have to be kidding." She glanced at Mary, her coworker and best friend. Mary snorted and leaned back on the couch.

"Quit being so dramatic. You wouldn't be a prostitute. You're simply an entertainer. A high-class, very expensive entertainer."

It wasn't a shock to know her best friend had contacts for this type of thing. Mary was known as the wild child all through high school. It was surprising that Mary actually presented it to her, though. Lalita didn't consider herself anything special physically, certainly not compared to Mary.

"I would be expected to have sex with total strangers." There was a hint of outrage and shock that laced Lalita's voice, but she didn't care. This had to be the most outrageous thing Mary had ever presented her with.

"Yeah, that's what makes it so much fun and why they're offering so much." Mary chuckled. "Listen, this is an exclusive offer, Lalita. I know you need the money, and this is a fast, safe way for you to acquire it. You wouldn't have to do anything but have sex and enjoy yourself for a couple of months. Believe me, the time flies, and you'll get just as much out of it as anyone else."

Lalita looked down at the crisp white card in her hand. It stated the details of what was expected of her, and how much was being offered. Her hands shook as she stared at dollar amount. It was an obscene amount of money, certainly enough to pay off all her debts and then have some left over. She glanced over her shoulder at the closed bedroom door.

"Don't worry about Lennon. I promise I'll take good care of him." Mary breathed out before continuing. "It's fucked up that Brad cheated on you with a girl barely out of high school, and it's even shittier that you got saddled with his debts, but this is the opportunity to get your life back."

Lalita swallowed and turned back around. She trusted Mary to care for her five-year-old son, but she couldn't help the guilt that assaulted her that she was considering leaving him for several months to go fuck people she didn't know, for money. Lalita thought about her ex-husband, the man that didn't want anything to do with their child even before he was born. It wasn't even so much that she cared that he left her, but the fact that he wanted nothing to do with Lennon was what enraged her. No matter how many hours she worked, she hadn't made a dent in the monumental debt Brad had so graciously left her to clean up.

"No pressure, hun. You do what you think is best, but you can't earn this kind of money working for Mr. Harris." Mary rose and grabbed her purse. "Listen, I got to run. You have the number if you decide to take the offer, but I wouldn't wait too long."

Lalita watched Mary leave. There was no surprise that Mary knew so much about this. Hell, her friend had probably participated in this kind of thing on more than one occasion.

When the door was shut, the silence caved in around her. She got up and walked over to her son's bedroom. She opened the door and stared at him as he slept. His chest rose and fell in even intervals, and his face was free of any worries or troubles the world offered. She closed the door and went over to the phone. Lalita stared down at the card once more and swallowed roughly. She may hate herself when everything was all said and done, but in the long run she needed to do what was best for her and her child. This may not be the most honest work, but the outcome and benefit outweighed her morals.

She picked up the receiver and dialed the number with shaky fingers. She reminded herself this wasn't a sure thing, anyway. There were a whole slew of preliminaries that had to be done before she was even offered the job. A tedious background and health check were just a few of the things she would be made to do. She wasn't old, but she was nearing thirty, and after having a child, her body didn't look like the eighteen-year-old girl Brad had left her for.

"Yes?"

She stood straighter and cleared her throat when someone picked up on the other end of the phone line. "Hello." Was that her voice, so shaky and uncertain? "I have a card and was told to call." She was vague, but then again Mary had told her that was all that she would need to say. There was a lengthy pause and then the deep male voice on the other end took her information and gave her instructions on what she was to do. After she hung up, she stared at the wall for a suspended moment. "I can't believe I am really going to do this."

* * * *

Lalita stood in front of six expensively dressed, hugely muscled, and extremely gorgeous men. Five of them sat behind a long, polished banquet table while the sixth stood behind them and nursed amber-colored liquor out of a square-cut glass. All of them eyed her quizzically. It had been three weeks since she decided she was going to go through with this. Not only had she gone through the grueling mental background check, she had also been poked and prodded as they deemed her "clean." When she found out she would be entertaining six men, she had nearly fainted with shock. Brad had been the one and only man she had ever been with sexually, and the idea of pleasuring six virile men was a little daunting.

She smoothed her sweaty hands down the plain, inexpensive sundress she bought the day before. She knew why she was at this house, knew that the men in front of her wanted to see what she could offer physically. She looked in each of their faces, all of them similar in looks, but different in their own way. The one at the far left appeared to be the leader. He had an air of authority when he spoke that the other five seemed to respect. She had instantly recognized his voice as the one she had spoken to when she made that initial call.

"Lalita Marshall?" Dorian, the one that seemed to be the leader, looked up from the folder that sat in front of him. She nodded nervously. "Let's skip the pleasantries. You know why you're here. He turned and looked at the other five men before continuing. "Why are you interested in working for us?"

Surprise filled her momentarily. He spoke so nonchalantly, like this was an everyday kind of job interview. She had assumed she would be ordered to remove her clothing. The fact that they actually wanted to know why she wanted the job embarrassed her. She swallowed and looked at each man.

"I…" She didn't know where to start. She could lie, but what was the point? "I need the money." When they all stayed silent, she continued. "I have a five-year-old son, and I need the money to take care of him." The men glanced at each other, and she wondered if she just ruined her chance. No doubt the idea of an older woman with a child turned them off. She threw back her shoulders and held her ground. She had been honest, but she hadn't been completely honest. There was no need for them to know that the reason she needed the money was not only to take care of her son, but because her ex-husband had left his debt solely in her hands.

There was something that flickered in Dorian's gaze. He leaned back in his chair and steepled his fingers. "I admire your honesty, Ms. Marshall. Let me introduce you to the rest of my associates." He started down the line with the man sitting next to him first. "This is Torryn, Kane, Zakary, and Aleck." He named the other men without taking his gaze from hers. "The man standing behind me is Michael."

Lalita smiled at each man. Michael gave her a once-over before turning his attention elsewhere. It was clear he wasn't impressed with her. They were all devilishly handsome, and the two at the end appeared to be younger than her.

"Now, enough with the casualties. Take your clothes off." Dorian's words were deep and low.

Lalita had expected this, but even so, her hands began to shake and her heart thundered in her chest. No one spoke or moved. All six men watched her with impassive and stoic expressions. *This is it. They'll either like what they see or send me packing.* She went for the buttons of her dress and slowly started to undo them. Maybe her nervousness would appear sensual? Not likely, since she considered herself the least sexual person on the planet.

When the buttons were undone, she slipped the material off her shoulders and let it pool at her feet. She had wanted to get some sexy lingerie, hoping the visual enticement would help her, but she hadn't been able to afford it. She wore a plain thong, nothing fancy but all she had. The bra she had on was white and cotton, the same as the thong. She could see each of their gazes roaming over her body, but none of them appeared to be affected by her near nudeness. She clasped her hands behind her back and felt her cheeks heat with embarrassment.

"Take all of it off, Ms. Marshall." Torryn spoke softly as he leaned back in his seat, the leather squeaking in protest to his massive form.

She unclasped her bra and let it fall to the floor. Despite having a child, her breasts were still pert and round. She was rather proud of them. Fingers hooked beneath the elastic of her thong, she pulled it slowly down her thighs. She kicked it aside and righted herself. Per their specific orders, her pussy was bare of any hair. The cool air wafted across her exposed cleft, and she fought back the shiver that threatened to spill forth. There were a couple of low coughs and some chairs squeaking as the men all shifted in their seats. Still their expressions showed nothing, so she couldn't gauge what they thought.

"Please, turn around." Aleck spoke, his voice just as deep as the others despite his youthful face.

She did as was asked and stared at the wall. She could feel their gazes on her ass and fought back the need to cover herself. It wasn't that she didn't like gorgeous men looking at her, but her body was certainly not that of a supermodel, which she was sure they were accustomed to.

"Spread your legs and grab your ankles without bending your knees."

Lalita didn't recognize the voice but did as she was asked regardless. Unused muscles stretched and protested, but she held the position. Blood rushed to her head as she held the position. She knew her pussy was on full display, knew her lips had spread open so they could see the pink of her cunt. A few murmurs sounded behind her, but she wasn't able to pick up on exactly what was being said. She held the position for what seemed like forever before another command was issued.

"You can straighten and turn back around."

Lalita felt slightly dizzy as the blood rushed from her head as she stood. She turned back around and straightened her shoulders. The five men seated all stared at her with stoic expressions. Michael moved around the table and circled her. Her heart started pounding even more frantically than it had been, by his close proximity. The smell of him, wild and potent, should have made her nervous not aroused.

He didn't touch her but didn't stop circling her either. No doubt he was really getting an eyeful. When he seemed satisfied with whatever he had been trying to find, he stopped in front of her and cupped her chin between his finger and thumb. They stared into each other's eyes, and Lalita felt her mouth go dry. Michael was impossibly handsome, but there was a mysterious quality to him that reflected outward.

"Thank you for your time. We have other ladies to interview today but will contact you if we are interested." Dorian's words were final, and they all turned toward each other and started murmuring. Michael let go of her chin and moved back behind the table. He didn't look at her again and neither did the other men.

She felt pushed to the side, disregarded even as she picked up her clothing and started putting it on. "Thank you for your time." The comment had been a passing thought more than anything else, and when she glanced up, she was surprised that all six watched her intently.

They didn't respond, just continued to look at her. An uncomfortable silence filled the room, and Lalita feared she had just done something terribly wrong. Maybe speaking out of turn or without permission was not allowed. It didn't matter anyway, not when she was pretty sure she was not going to be offered the job. She grabbed her purse and left the house without a backward glance. She had totally fucked that up.

Chapter Two

A week passed, and Lalita hadn't heard anything from her six would-be employers. Desperation and disappointment weren't even the right words she would have used for how she felt. Even though she had originally been unsure of even taking the job, the idea that she probably would not get hired left her feeling depressed. The financial strain had been taking its toll on her, but when the very thought that she could get out from under the monumental debt she had been left with presented itself, there had been a small spark of hope. Even that was now starting to dwindle away like an extinguished flame. It seemed like no matter how much she worked overtime, she never made enough money. Living paycheck to paycheck was starting to get really old and frustrating.

She washed the rest of the dinner dishes and dried her hands. She leaned against the counter and watched Lennon stack colored blocks. As hard as her life was, she wouldn't change it for anything, not when she had her baby. The phone rang and drew her out of her musings.

"Hello?"

"Ms. Marshall?"

That voice, Dorian's, so deep and commanding, washed through her and made her instantly dizzy. She closed her eyes and willed her heart to slow down. As she listened to him speak, she had to sit down because her legs became unsteady. She hung the phone up and stared at the chipped Formica counter.

"Momma?"

Her son's small voice drew her out of her thoughts, and she smiled down at him. Both of their lives were about to change. They had chosen her. Out of all the women they "interviewed," she was the one they wanted to entertain them. The guilt was still an emotion that came into play, especially as she stared at her baby, but she couldn't deny that the money she would earn would help her and Lennon out immensely. Yes, their lives were certainly going to change, but only for the better.

* * * *

The one thing Lalita was thankful for was that Lennon hadn't cried when she said good-bye. He had actually been happy to spend time with his auntie Mary. She now stood in front of two massive oak doors that were attached to a monstrous mansion. The building looked like it should be on a hilltop in Scotland, not an hour from the place she called home. She put her small suitcase in her other sweaty hand and knocked on the door.

A limo had picked her up and dropped her off in front of the mansion. The driver hadn't said two words to her, but it didn't matter because she doubted she could have held a conversation anyway. She took a step back and waited as trepidation pounded through her.

The door opened a moment later to reveal Kane, one of the two younger-looking males she had met only a short time ago. His light blond hair and bright blue eyes made him appear as young as she assumed him to be. Although she was most likely older, his physique didn't indicate this, as he was taller, more muscular, and definitely all male. Her mouth went dry as she watched his eyes travel up and down her body. Despite the emotions coursing through her, she felt her pussy start to become moist and tingle.

"Lalita." He all but purred her name as he stepped aside and gestured for her to enter.

He took her bag and placed his hand on the small of her back as he led her farther into the house. There was so much heat coming from that one small touch that she thought she would burn alive. The interior was just as magnificent as the exterior. Marble flooring, shining dark wood, and a crystal chandelier were just a few of the amenities that made up the foyer. Never had Lalita seen such beauty. Her small and cramped two-bedroom apartment looked like a Cracker Jack box compared to this place.

"Lovely, isn't it?" Kane's deeply whispered voice brushed across the shell of her ear.

She shivered and turned to look at him. They were stopped in the middle of the foyer, his height causing her to crane her head back to see into his face. "Yes." Was that her voice? All breathy and sensual? She swallowed and took a step back.

"This way." The playfulness that had just graced his features disappeared as he ushered her into a large living room.

The other five men stood in front of a large fireplace, and although it wasn't lit, their body heat seemed to warm the entire room. She had had plenty of time to think about what this whole situation meant and entailed, but she couldn't deny that standing before six powerful and masculine men, knowing what she would be doing with them, was an aphrodisiac that caused her pussy to become even more saturated and her nipples to harden.

"Please, have a seat, Ms. Marshall." Dorian gestured to one of the plush chairs.

"Lalita. Please call me Lalita." She didn't think there was any reason for them not to be on a first name basis. After all, her main job here was to make sure each and every one of them was well satisfied. She sat down and stared at Dorian. His expression showed nothing, but he nodded in agreement.

"We will set down some ground rules first. You have already signed the contract, so these shouldn't be new to you, but I want to make sure everything is clear while you are employed by my associates and me." He took a step back and leaned against the mantle just as Torryn stepped forward and spoke.

"While you can always say 'no' to any of our requests, you must know that by doing so you are forfeiting any and all money."

She knew everything they expected of her, had gone through what they expected of her with a fine-tooth comb. Some of the things hadn't shocked her, but there were several that had her eyes growing wide and her mouth going dry. She nodded her understanding and swallowed. Torryn stepped back, and Kane started to speak.

"While here, you will be expected to make sure each of us is satisfied. Although we will initiate acts ourselves, you are expected to take things into your own hands from time to time. We should never be left wanting."

Aleck was the next to speak, the youngest-looking of the six, and almost-innocent seeming. "You will have your own room on the second floor, as will each of us. Any night is fair game for us, although we aren't ignorant to the fact you will need a day of alone time to do as you please.".The other five men stood behind him, so they didn't see him smile or wink at her. He was definitely the more easygoing out of the six.

When Michael stepped forward, Lalita took an involuntary step back. Whereas Dorian seemed to be the leader of the group, there was a dark, mysterious quality about Michael that drew her to him as well as frightened her. "Your pussy is to always be shaved and oiled. If it is not, we reserve the right to punish you as we see fit. You must also be ready to accept us. If you are not, we will assume you no longer wish to fulfill your part of the deal."

"We aren't slave drivers by any means, but we do expect certain things while you are here." Zakary spoke loud and clear, his dominant voice brooking no arguments.

She knew what punishment they spoke of. She had read all about the dominant and submissive roles they expected her to adhere to. Lalita knew she could pull off the submissive role to a tee. Hell, she had been Brad's doormat for longer than she cared to admit.

"As part of the agreement, you are not to turn any of us down. Condoms may be used at any of our discretion, but it is not required." Dorian's voice was like an auditory orgasm, and she fought back the tremors of arousal. All of their voices did something to her, but Dorian's voice had this certain tenor that seemed to caress each of her nerve endings.

"You are expected to stay here the entire time. At the end of the contract, you will get the amount offered in full." Dorian leaned casually against the mantle, his dark gaze settled on her. "Are the rules clear, Lalita?"

The way he said her name was like a slap on her clit. She took a deep breath and nodded. None of what they said was a surprise, but the intensity with which it was said was.

Everyone was so still and silent for so long that Lalita's nerves started to unravel. Michael took a step toward her and ran his finger down her neck. She was sure the touch hadn't meant to be sexual, but the way his calloused finger smoothed down her throat and stopped at her pounding pulse sent a warm gush of fluid to slip from her pussy.

Michael leaned in so that their lips were mere inches apart. "You will be shown to your room and have an hour to get your belongings in order and to prepare yourself." The air in Lalita's lungs stilled as his words finally penetrated her mind.

"You have brought a bag, although I believe it was stated that you were to bring nothing. Everything you need for the next couple of months is already in your room." Dorian's words had her turning her head away from Michael's almost-hypnotic gaze. As she watched Dorian push off the wall, she felt Michael step away from her. Already she was needy and wanting whatever they could give her. Dorian stopped in front of her and picked up her suitcase. He held his hand out for her to take it.

It was true she was told not to bring anything, but there were some things a woman couldn't leave home without. She expected the other five to follow, but as Dorian and she left the room, no one else joined them. Neither of them spoke as they made the journey, which Lalita was starting to feel was to the very gates of hell itself.

When they reached the top of the stairs, he started pointing out each of their rooms. She wasn't surprised to see that all of the men would be staying on the same hall as her. Hell, that brought a whole new meaning to the word "easy access." When Dorian led her into her room, she couldn't help how her mouth dropped open in awe. Navy blue and black silk adorned the bed. The dark satin curtains and fixtures looked like they belonged to a queen.

"The dresser and armoire hold what you are expected to wear while here. The bathroom is over there," Dorian pointed to a small door off to the side. "I've already set out what you are to wear for entertaining tonight." He pointed to the bed. She turned and looked at the scraps of lace and silk that lay atop the plush comforter.

Before she could utter a word, she heard the bedroom door shut. Lalita stared at the closed door before sitting on the mattress and looking at her surroundings. She had no idea how she was going to satisfy all of them when she apparently hadn't been able to satisfy one man. Brad had made it perfectly clear she had been the worst lay he had ever had. There hadn't been anyone in her life since Brad, which meant a whopping five years of nothing sexual. Lalita just hoped she could physically handle six strapping men.

As she thought of them, Lalita couldn't help but picture their hugely muscled frames and brooding good looks. There was no doubt in her mind that their cocks were just as impressive as the rest of their bodies. The very thought had her pussy clenching in fear but also becoming wet in excitement. Brad had been anything but well endowed, and the very thought of taking on all six men was something that sent a shiver of awareness through her.

It was nice that they had given her a little bit of time to herself, but she realized that that time also had her thinking of every fear that this little endeavor entailed. Nervousness and anxiety clashed inside of her, and she knew that if she fucked this up, she wouldn't only be screwing her life over, she would also be hurting her child's.

There was no sense in worrying about what could or couldn't happen. Pushing those thoughts aside, Lalita explored the room first, starting with the huge armoire. She walked up to it and gripped the carved brass handles and pulled it open. Shock and amazement held her temporarily paralyzed. Dozens of lacy, barely-there outfits hung from silk-padded hangers. Her hands shook as she lifted them to run her fingers through the exquisite material. Some were more traditional, but there were others that downright scared the shit out of her. Leather straps, clamps, and strips of silk hung from some of the more racy pieces and had her throat drying. *How in the hell do they expect me to wear some of these things?*

She closed the doors, knowing that the less she analyzed them, the better she would be. The smell of lavender and lemon filled her senses, and she ran her fingers over everything before stopping in front of the only window in the room. The sun was starting to set and washed everything in muted hues of pinks, yellows, and oranges. Her room overlooked a beautiful courtyard and even an impressive hedge maze. The colors of the flowers and the brightness of the green grass were a cacophony of stimulation to her senses.

Knowing she only had a limited amount of time, Lalita decided she better get the primping out of the way. True, they had already chosen her for the job, but she still needed to look her best if she planned on keeping them satisfied and ensuring her position here. She went into the bathroom and switched on the light. Pristine white tile surrounded her, along with a bathtub that she didn't doubt would fit all seven of them. Heart thundering behind her ribs, Lalita undressed.

Chapter Three

As Lalita stood in just a towel, water slipping down her exposed limbs from her recent bath, she couldn't help the paralyzed feeling that slammed into her at that exact moment. As she reached for the outfit they expected her to wear, her bedroom door opened, which had her turning around in surprise. Michael stood in the threshold, his eyes trained on her with so much intensity she had to take a step back.

He didn't say anything, just stepped farther into her bedroom, shut the door behind him, and moved toward her. He looked like some kind of wild animal stalking her.

"The others don't know I'm here, so we'll make sure to keep this our little secret." His voice, so deep and baritone, surrounded her.

His appearance was the same as the others, tall, dark, and extremely handsome, but the way he presented himself was as if he knew he could have her at any moment and planned on doing just that.

He stood a foot from her and reached out to grip her towel. Although she was so nervous, she let the material fall to the ground unceremoniously. As she stood there completely nude, nipples hard because of the chill in the air, she was acutely aware of the scorching look he gave her.

Michael curled his hand around her neck, brought her close enough that her bare breasts pressed against his solid chest, and kissed her like she was oxygen and he was suffocating. Stunned wasn't even the right word to describe how she felt at that moment. For a split second she stood there stiff, not knowing what to do from his unexpected advance, but when he swept his tongue along her bottom lip, she instantly melted into him.

She opened her mouth and met his tongue with hers. He tasted spicy and addicting, like nothing she had ever experienced before. It was exhilarating. For several long minutes they continued to kiss, and although she wished he would have touched her body, he kept one hand on the nape of her neck and the other on her shoulder. He was just as aroused as she was, because his erection pressed insistently against her belly.

When he stepped away, Lalita swayed on her feet. She felt drugged. He gave her body a once-over, smirked devilishly, and turned around and left. Lalita stared at her now-closed door for a long moment, not able to get her brain to focus enough to know what she was supposed to do next. Her cunt was soaked, and her nipples were so hard and sensitive she had to grit her teeth in frustration. Was this all part of their master plan? To tempt her but not deliver what she really wanted? If so, this was going to be one hell of a long time here.

When she was finally able to get herself composed, Lalita took a deep breath and adjusted the miniscule thong she wore. Her bedroom door closed softly behind her, and as the silence surrounded her, she could hear the pounding of her heart. The stairs stood in front of her like an omen of what was to come. Taking those tentative steps toward them, her knees wobbled. Not only did they expect her to wear five-inch heels, the outfit they'd picked out didn't cover her ass, pussy, or even her tits. She admitted it held no real purpose other than visual pleasure, but knowing little more than scraps of lace wrapped around her body had her feeling more sexual than she ever had.

She descended the stairs cautiously, knowing that with her luck she'd trip and seriously hurt herself, which would put her out of commission. Loud male laughter broke the silence, and she stepped onto the landing. Her breasts bounced with every step she took, and she stopped right before she entered the room where all the noise came from. Another deep breath did nothing to calm her nerves. She glanced down at herself once more and groaned internally.

The lace and leather straps wrapped around her abdomen and pushed her breasts up. Her nipples were hard, poking straight out as if they sought a mouth. She could see her bare pussy, could even see the swell of her labia and the pinkness of her flesh. The bath, and especially Michael, had done nothing to calm her nerves, instead racking up her arousal higher until her body felt itchy and tight.

The deep male voices that were only a few short feet from her went straight to her clit. These men were strangers to her, yet here she was, about to walk in practically naked and fuck their brains out. *This is it, Lalita. Go in there, rock their worlds, and earn the money that you and Lennon need.*

She stepped around the corner and found she couldn't take another step. A fire was lit, and all six of them milled around casually. Square-cut glasses filled with amber-colored liquid were in some of their hands while others held long-neck bottles of beer. Dorian glanced toward the open doorway as if he sensed her, and all conversation ceased. A few muffled coughs sounded, and she found the strength to take another step into the room. She could see each and every one of their eyes roaming over her body, and the thought alone had her pussy tingling and becoming even more saturated. Knowing she had men such as these, men who were gorgeous and physically perfect, made her feel sexy, wanted, and even needed

"Holy. Fuck."

Those two words, uttered deep and scratchy, had her darting her attention to Torryn. Cheeks heating immediately from the obscenity, Lalita couldn't help but notice the massive erection that was pressed against his slacks. The need to shift nervously under his gaze was almost unbearable. Although Torryn was the first to speak, Zakary was the first to approach her. She held her ground as he made a slow circle around her. Eyes lowered, Lalita was almost afraid to look at him as he "assessed her." The feeling of fingers trailing along the exposed skin of her arm caused her to shiver.

"Look at you now, all pretty and ready for us." Zakary spoke close to her ear, his warm, whiskey-scented breath trailing along her senses and making her feel weak with need. His finger lifted her chin, and she was forced to look into his deep green eyes. His youthful appearance didn't deter from the fact that he wanted her or that he knew exactly what he was doing.

He moved in closer and pressed his body flush with hers. His arms wrapped around her, and she felt the hard length of his cock press against her belly. Hands shaking, she didn't know if she should play the good submissive and wait for his orders, or if she should lift her hands and touch him as well. The idea of running her fingers over his body enticed her, but in the end she kept her hands at her side.

When she licked her lips, a nervous habit she was coming to find out about, Zakary's gaze dropped down to the movement and his lids grew heavy with arousal. Lalita felt his hands smooth up and down her back, and her flesh tightened. When the tops of his fingers skimmed her ass, she felt herself tense, not from fear, but from something darker and needier.

Hand now planted firmly on one of the mounds, he massaged the globe while his other hand started to undo the lacing in the back of the lingerie she wore. The knowledge that there were five other men in the room watching this did not escape her. Although it aroused her to a degree, she admitted to herself that it also made her feel uneasy and slightly uncomfortable.

Before Lalita could assimilate what Zakary's intentions were, his mouth slanted across hers and his tongue speared into her mouth. He tasted different than Michael, and whereas Michael had seemed to make love to her more, Zakary kissed her with aggression. It was a startling but welcome contrast. There was a part of her that couldn't help but melt at his dominance. Soon he had her top unlaced, and she was vaguely aware of it falling to the ground. Her nipples rubbed against the material of his shirt, causing them to stiffen and elongate even further.

When she felt his hands slip between her ass cheeks and run along the saturated folds of her pussy, she gasped against his mouth. As if the sound triggered something inside of him, he broke the kiss and took a step away from her. Her pussy tingled from the barely-there touch he delivered, and it felt as if every cell in her body was sparking with electricity.

As her brain slowly started to function once again, Lalita looked around the room at each man. Their hard composure seemed slightly strained, and if the way their cocks pressed against their pants was anything to go by, they enjoyed the show.

"Come here."

Knees threatening to give out, she made determined steps toward Dorian. It was paramount that she show these men she could handle what they had to give. There was a moment of hushed silence, and when she stopped in front of Dorian, she noticed the other five left the room. When the door shut behind the last person, she made sure to keep her head lowered, reminding herself continuously that he was the dominant and she the submissive. Her heart slammed hard against her sternum, but despite her anxiousness, she was aroused beyond belief. She could feel her own wetness coat her labia and start to slide down her inner thighs.

There was a long pause before Dorian finally spoke. "Look at me, Lalita."

She lifted her gaze, not knowing what to expect. He looked like a warrior standing beside the roaring fire, like a solider ready to defeat his next conquest. His dark hair and eyes made him seem hard, unreasonable, like a king waiting for his prize. A gush of moisture left her cunt at the thought. Just a look from him, a silent, demanding gaze, had her so ready to be fucked she feared she would pass out once he finally entered her.

He moved over to one of the chairs and sat down. He didn't speak, just watched her as he slowly gestured for her to come forward with a curl of his finger. When she was before him, he started to undo his slacks.

"On your knees." The words weren't gentle or coaxing. He demanded them. Never had she thought giving head would make her so excited. She wanted to feel his cock in her mouth, wanted to taste every dip and hollow and imprint it in her memory.

When his cock was free, she felt her eyes widen. He was massive, thick and long and already seeping pre-cum. She didn't know why she was surprised by his size. He was, after all, a very large man, so it would be reasonable that every part of his body was just as impressive.

Lalita dropped to her knees between his splayed thighs and stared at the monster staring right at her. Where was she even supposed to start? Right before she took the head in her mouth, she breathed out deeply. A slight movement to her side caught her attention, and she saw how Dorian's hand shook ever so slightly. Maybe she was making a bigger impression the she thought.

She had only given a blow job a few times, and both times Brad had acted less than pleased with her performance. Then again, it wasn't as if Brad had given her much to work with.

The thick crest of Dorian's cock nudged at her lips, and she opened wide to suck the head inside. He tasted salty and all male. She sucked harder and started to move down the thick, long length. What she couldn't engulf with her mouth, she gripped with her hand. She started to suck feverishly while she stroked what she couldn't reach. Her jaw ached, but she didn't care. The pain was a welcome feeling that she hoped steamed off some of her arousal.

"You are not permitted to come unless I say you can."

She paused momentarily and flicked her eyes up to his face. He appeared nonplused. Even though climaxing seemed heavenly, she was surprised that satisfying him overrode even that need. Although she amended she was extremely aroused, she didn't actually think she could come just from giving head. His comment gave her strength, a need to please him not just so she could get off, but because she wanted him to find pleasure, wanted to taste his cum slide down her throat.

As if she was a mad woman, she pumped her mouth harder and faster down his erection until her mouth burned. The temptation to slip her hand between her legs and stroke her clit a few times became more demanding, and she wondered if Dorian knew this would be her reaction the whole time.

The urge to moan in desire and frustration became lodged in her throat. Just then, a small squirt of hot cum filled her mouth, and she couldn't hold back the whimpering noise then. He was close. She knew this with certainty. His body was tense, and she could feel his cock grow harder in her mouth. Using her other hand to cup his impressive balls, she rolled them around in her palm, and that seemed to be his breaking point. Hot, salty semen filled her mouth, and she eagerly swallowed it. The noise that came from her was almost a pleading cry. Surprisingly, her orgasm was just out of her reach. His hands speared into her hair, and his hips lifted up slightly, pushing his cock deeper into her mouth until the tip hit the back of her throat and she gagged.

When his shaft started to grow soft in her mouth, she pulled back and licked her lips. He only looked at her once before adjusting his clothing, getting out of the chair, and leaving the room. She knelt on the floor and stared at the closed door, stunned. Before she had time to contemplate what had just happened, the door was opened, and Torryn walked in. He had the swagger of a man who knew he was about to get off. He stopped in front of her, unzipped his pants, and pulled his heavy erection out. He was just as large as Dorian and equally as intimidating. She rose up on her knees and steadied her palms against his muscular thighs.

Her body was on fire, and she prayed he let her come, prayed he repaid her in kind.

She took his cock in her mouth and started to suck him slowly at first. That didn't seem to appease him, because all too soon he was thrusting in her mouth quickly. She hummed around his shaft and started to move her hand between her legs. Before she could even stroke her clit once, Torryn's gruff words stopped her.

"I haven't given you permission to touch yourself. Because you took it upon yourself to attempt to do so, you will be punished by not being permitted to come."

She could have cried at that moment. Her clit was impossibly engorged and tingled every time it rubbed against her pussy lips. Frustration filled her, but she was determined to satisfy him, needing to taste him as she had tasted Dorian. He started to fuck her mouth like a man starving, a man needing to get off as much as she did. She caressed his balls, and like Dorian, he, too, came seconds later.

Lalita swallowed his cum with relish, but just like the man before him, he said nothing as he tucked himself back in his pants and left the room. She stared in shock at his departing form. Her clit pulsed and her nipples begged for attention. Her knees started to hurt, so she stood. The door opened a moment later, and Kane, Michael, Aleck, and Zakary stepped in.

Kane and Zakary flanked her and immediately while Aleck and Michael moved off to the side. Kane and Zakary started to touch her nipples and pussy. Their fingers were like magic, stroking and plucking, bringing her to a new height until she was right on the precipice of climax. They stopped all too soon, and she sagged in disappointment.

"Don't worry, baby. This is going to feel so good." Zakary's words were spoken softly and with a hint of playfulness.

She looked at him, his deep green eyes and blond hair adding a boy-next-door appearance despite the hard muscles and massive height. They led her over to the couch, and Zakary immediately started tweaking her nipples. Each time he pulled her nipple, she had to bite her lip to keep from begging him for more. Kane shifted behind her, and when he was seated, he pulled her on top of his lap. She glanced up at Zakary, hoping she could gauge his intentions by his expression but realizing it was no use. All six men held steel-like composures.

Kane positioned her legs so they were draped over his thighs. He spread his own legs wide, which in turn caused hers to stretch to the point that she could feel unused muscles straining. Zakary started to undo his pants, and Kane did the same, moving his hands between their bodies and pulling his cock free from the zipper. Both of their dicks sprang forth, hard, long and flushed red with need. Her mouth watered, her clit throbbed, and her nipples tingled at the sight.

Lalita felt Kane kiss the side of her throat and then looked down to see him stroke himself. His knuckles would gently brush against her cunt folds, and she shivered at the feel. Zakary did the same, stroking his cock with easy, unhurried movements while his eyes stayed trained on her pussy. He took a step forward and brushed the tip of his cock against her mouth. The silky head moved along her closed lips, teasing her, urging her to open. She felt his sticky pre-cum spread along her lips, and she couldn't hold back any longer.

When she opened her mouth, Zakary shoved his shaft into the waiting warmth. After sucking two men off only moments before, Lalita assumed she would be immune to the arousal that it caused within her, but how wrong she was. Zakary tasted different than Torryn and Dorian, and she found she grew just as excited giving him head as she had with the other two.

Closing her eyes and absorbing the taste and feel of Zakary, Lalita snapped her eyes open a moment later when she felt Kane brush his knuckles along her pussy. His fingers spread her moisture around and brought it to her clit. He rubbed the small bud slowly at first, but he seemed to match his movements with how fast she sucked Zakary's cock.

Soon she was rocking gently on his lap. Back and forth she moved, faster and harder until she felt a delicious burn start to travel throughout her whole body. Just as she would have exploded with pleasure, Kane removed his fingers. She didn't stop sucking despite the impasse she was faced with.

Kane shifted her thighs so they were no longer spread wide. He wedged his cock between her legs, so the length of his cock rested right against her cunt. He started to move so that his cock pumped in and out of her clenched thighs. Her labia wrapped around the hard flesh, and with every pump of his dick her clit was teased. They had to have done this before, because it took skill to perform a sexual act such as this. Not once did Kane's movements jar her from blowing Zakary.

Her pussy cream had his cock slipping against her skin with ease. She gripped Zakary's thighs as pleasure pulsed through her. She was so close to coming she could taste it, could see the flash of lights getting ready to explode behind her eyelids.

Just like that flash of lights she expected to see, Zakary exploded. His cum filled her mouth and slipped down her throat. Lalita drank it all and moaned with relish at the distinct flavor of him. Kane was soon to follow. He gripped her waist tightly, gave a ragged groan, and pressed his forehead against her back as his cock jerked. Hot, thick semen pumped out of his cock and landed on her thighs and pussy. The sensation of both men coming because of her was almost enough to get her off, almost.

Zakary's semi-hard cock slipped free of her mouth, and he stepped away. Kane lifted her off of him, grabbed a rag that conveniently lay on the table beside them, and cleaned her off. Out of breath and heart racing, Lalita stared at the two of them. She closed her eyes and tried to get her bearings. They had said it would feel so good, and they were right, for them. She was still on edge. Someone gave her nipple a tight tug, and she snapped her eyes open. The bud was already hard and sensitive, and when they pulled on it, pleasure slammed straight to her clit. Only two more to go.

With her eyes still closed, Lalita sensed someone standing right in front of her. When she was finally able to open her eyes, she saw that it was Michael. He gave her a knowing smile and held his hand out for her to take. The moment she was standing he turned her around and brought her back flush with his chest. Aleck stood on the other side of the couch, cock in hand and eyes half lidded.

When Michael started kissing the side of her neck, she couldn't help but let her head fall back and rest on his shoulder. It felt so good having his lips move sensuously along her throat. His hands on her breasts were next. He cupped the globes that seemed too heavy and curled his fingers around her flesh. His hard cock was pressed between the crease of her ass, and because she just couldn't help herself, Lalita pressed her bottom firmly against his shaft. His response was a gentle bite on the nape of her neck.

"You naughty girl." Michael spoke low enough that she knew Aleck hadn't heard.

He moved them over to a recliner, and although it was somewhat an awkward trek, he never once stopped kissing her or touching her breasts. Her thighs brushed against the back of the leather chair, and a moment later he was using his hand on the middle of her back to push her forward. With her upper body hanging over the chair and her ass thrust forward, she couldn't help but wonder what his intentions were. The position made it so that she was eyelevel with Aleck's shaft.

Mesmerized by the sight of Aleck pumping his fist along the hardened length, she brought her eyes up until she was staring into his eyes. As she stared into his eyes, she felt Michael spread her ass cheeks. Something cold and wet slid between her cheeks, and she instantly tensed. Would he really fuck her in the ass right now? It was a frightening thought but also tantalizing.

"Relax, honey, tonight there won't be any penetration." Michael's seductively whispered words brushed across her ear. Had her body language been that transparent that he had known what she was thinking?

He moved his finger over her anus, and she tensed once again. "Just watch Aleck." Michael smoothed the lube over the hole a few times before removing his finger and gripping her thigh. He lifted her leg and placed her foot on the arm of the recliner. The position caused her pussy to be on full display.

She didn't miss how Aleck's gaze dipped to her exposed slit or how his eyes seemed to drop even lower until she could barely see his irises.

Michael moved his hand around her middle and rested it on her bare mound. With his index and middle fingers, he spread her pussy lips until chilled air wafted across her exposed inner labia's. She could feel his cock nestled between the slick crease of her ass and knew what he planned on doing. He was going to get off while helping Aleck get off with a little visual entertainment.

Michael started thrusting into her ass slowly at first, but with each passing moment his speed increased. "Reach between your legs and play with that swollen little clit. Rub it hard and fast and keep your eyes locked with Aleck's."

Lalita did just that. She had to bite her bottom lip for fear of coming all too soon. It felt so good, and with the arousal inside of her slowly building until she thought she couldn't take it any longer, she knew that if they didn't give her permission to come, she wouldn't be able to stop herself.

Michael's thrusting became faster and faster until he was panting heavily behind her. He bit the back of her neck gently at first, but soon those little love bites were turning into stings that only seemed to heighten her desire.

Aleck's fist was a blur of flesh as he stroked his cock. He never took his eyes off her pussy, and that fact coupled with the feel of Michael's heavy shaft teasing the sensitive tissue of her anus had her whole body tingling. As if they knew she was perilously close to climaxing, Aleck groaned deeply.

"Fuck, baby. Your clit is so red and swollen. I just want to bury my head between your thighs and suck it until you come in my mouth." Aleck's words had her orgasm racing toward the surface, but when Michael bit the spot where her shoulder and neck met and a pain blossomed in that area, her climax receded.

"That's it, honey. Moan for us." Michael's words penetrated her mind. She hadn't realized she had been making any noises, but now that he brought it to her attention, she was acutely aware that small mewling noises came from her.

Deep male grunts and groans filled the room. Michael took his free hand and cupped her breast. He tweaked the nipple until it stood hard and elongated. Perspiration covered both of them, and the feel of his sweat-slicked chest moving sexually along her sweat-slicked back was highly erotic.

"Oh God, Lalita. Here I come." Michael bit her shoulder again, and she felt his hot cum cover her pussy and inner thighs. She kept her eyes trained on Aleck, kept rubbing her clit, hoping he, too, would come just as hard as Michael did.

Michael rested his head on her back when his orgasm ended. She was surprised when he kissed the back of her head and stepped away from her. Aleck had stopped stroking himself and now just stared at her while panting hard. Michael cleaned off his cum from her body with a warm rag, and a moment later she heard the door shut as he left.

A hushed second of silence descended upon them. Aleck, the youngest-looking male in the bunch, moved closer to her until he stood mere inches from her body. His blond hair was slightly longer than the other five men's, and his green eyes seemed so bright they glowed. She tried to get up, but her legs were so weak. He skimmed his eyes over her nude body. His cock grew was still hard and long, and she couldn't help but lick her lips. *When had she become such a lush?*

When she flicked her gaze back to his, she saw that he was staring at her breasts. The heat and arousal was high in the room, so thick that it was tangible.

"Damn, baby. You don't know how bad I want to fuck you right now." His voice was a deep growl, feral and almost aggressive. It seemed to be contradictive to his almost-innocent appearance.

They were both naked, their body heat bouncing between each other, their lust mixing together. He looked just as good as the rest, all tanned, toned flesh, muscles bulging in all the right places, and a cock that had her pussy clenching in worry and her heart speeding in excitement. His shaft, thick, stiff, and an angry red, had her mouth watering in anticipation.

Shock filtered through her when Aleck gently placed his hands on her shoulder and pushed her onto the recliner. He gripped each of her legs and placed them over the arms of the chair so her pussy lips spread open right in front of his face. He dropped to his knees in front of her and placed both hands on her inner thighs. She squirmed because of his close proximity. His hot, moist breath teased her folds, and her breathing hitched. That simple stream of air along her engorged clit had her body heating further. His gaze went to her breasts, and then one of his hands followed. He massaged the globes, tweaking the nipples until they were poker straight and straining forward.

He attacked her pussy then, licking and sucking with such force she couldn't stop herself from throwing her head back and moaning. He let go of her breast and trailed his hand down her belly. She lifted her head and looked down at him, watching in a sexual high as he pulled her pussy lips apart with his thumbs, blew warm air across her exposed cleft, and went back to devouring her. Her clit stuck out, the tiny bud hard and red, aching for attention. As if he read her mind, her suctioned his mouth around it, sucking so hard she couldn't breathe.

On and on he went, sucking, nipping, licking until she couldn't take it anymore and was begging him to stop. She thrashed her head, tried to push him away, but he was relentless.

"Oh God, please stop or let me come. Let me come, please let me come." Lalita prayed he let her, prayed he was more merciful then the last five. As if her words finally sunk into his brain, he stopped his ministrations, and she breathed out wearily. *Oh God.*

He watched her for a moment, his mouth red and glistening from her pussy juice, and stood. He offered her his hand, and she accepted. He led her over to the fireplace, but she was slow to keep up. Her legs felt like pudding. When he stopped in front of the fire and gently laid her atop the plush rug, she didn't know what his plans were.

This was completely different than what the other five had done. He pushed her back and covered her body with his. The feel of his hard cock against her cunt was a torture all in itself.

His mouth latched onto the column of her throat, and he started to slowly lick and suck at her flesh. His hips started to slowly pump into hers, his cock rubbing along the sensitive nerve endings of her clit and making her wetter. Her legs were spread wide as he continued to pump against her.

"Wrap your legs around my waist."

There was no hesitation on her part at his request. Legs now around his waist, she tilted her head more to the side, her skin growing tight with sensitivity as he laved her flesh. If she lifted her hips just a little higher and tilted her pelvis just so, she could lodge the head of his cock into her cunt. She went to do just that, needing to feel a big dick stuffing her to ease the burn within her. He sensed where her thoughts were going, though, because his hand on her hip stilled her movements.

He ran his tongue up her neck and over the shell of her ear. "Not tonight, baby," he whispered in her ear and brought his other hand to her breast. "Soon I'll get you all to myself, and it's going to feel so good."

His words had her shivering. His palm rasped over her nipple, and his whole body tensed above hers. His pumping hips picked up momentum, and she knew he was close. He tugged at her nipple and then grunted before she felt the hot jets of his cum pulse between her thighs and down her ass. He stayed with her far longer than any of the others, just holding, stroking, and caressing her. When he left, she stayed in front of the fire, her thoughts wayward, her body feeling not like her own. *This is going to be the longest and hardest two months of my life.*

Chapter Four

The next day wasn't any different than the one before. At every opportunity, the men found ways to stroke, caress, and tease Lalita's body until she was on the verge of begging to be fucked, but she was always left wanting. She felt like a wanton female because all she could think about was them fucking her, shoving their cocks in her pussy until she couldn't walk.

As lunch arrived she was offered a small reprieve from their touches. She ate quickly and used the rest of the time to explore the mansion. The place was monstrous, far too large for a household of only six. Most of the doors were locked, and although she was curious what lay behind them, there were plenty of other attractions in the mansion to keep her occupied.

She found herself walking down a lavish hallway. She had made so many turns she could honestly say she was lost. When she finally stopped and looked around, she tried to decipher how to get back to the main part of the house. A light above her caught her attention, and she turned to stare at a silver-framed photo mere inches from her face. The picture was of her six Masters and an older man and woman. It wasn't hard to come to the conclusion that the people in the photo were all related. The resemblance was just too uncanny.

"That is an old photo."

Lalita spun around and gasped as she looked into Dorian's face. She took a step back and bumped into a small end table, which in turn caused the vase atop it to crash to the floor and shatter. Horror filled her at the destruction she had just caused. When she turned around and looked down to survey the damage, she stepped on a shard of ceramic.

The jagged piece sliced into the bottom of her stocking-clad foot, and she cried out in pain. The heels she was to wear at all times hung in her hands. She now regretted taking them off.

"Fuck, I didn't mean to frighten you." She was in Dorian's arms an instant later, her legs draped over his forearms as he cradled her body close to his.

"I am so sorry about the vase." It probably cost a fortune. He didn't seem to pay attention to what she said, though. Lalita looked at her foot, which was leaving a trail of blood in its wake as he carried her into a room. The wound hurt terribly, but the idea that she had most likely broken a priceless heirloom and probably lost the money she would have earned was more painful.

"I'm more worried about your foot. Let's get it cleaned before you get an infection." His voice had a deep timbre, actually holding a note of concern in it.

When he set her on a plush bed, she couldn't help but stare around at the opulent room. It was no surprise that the room was just as lavish as all the others she had seen thus far. Light blue silk embroidered with gold thread was the main form of décor, along with photos of women in eighteenth-century attire.

Dorian gently pushed her back on the bed and propped her foot up with one of the pillows. "I'll be back in a minute."

He left a moment later, and Lalita breathed out. She was astutely aware that the position had her pussy lips plumped out in full few. Adjusting the outfit as much as she could, she managed to cover a small part of her vagina. Not that it mattered, since they had all seen what she looked like, but the idea of Dorian tending to her foot while her pussy was right in his face seemed almost inappropriate.

Surveying the cut once again, she amended it didn't look too severe. True to his word, Dorian entered a moment later. He held a black leather bag in his hand and pulled up a chair in front of her foot.

She watched in awe as he cut away the stocking, cleaned the blood off, and assessed the wound.

"The good news is it isn't deep enough to where you'd need sutures, but the bad news is it'll hurt like a bitch." He glanced up at her and smiled. "We'll have to make sure you stay off your feet."

The double entendre had her blushing fiercely. She had no doubt he could follow through with that promise. The bag by her leg looked like one of those old-fashioned leather bags doctors used to carry. He pulled bandages, a bottle of clear liquid, and a tube of ointment out of it.

"You can talk, Lalita." He smirked but didn't take his attention off her foot. "You aren't a prisoner here."

His words put her at ease, but only marginally. "What is all that stuff?"

He started to wrap white gauze around her foot. "I cleaned the wound with alcohol, and the cream is just antibiotic ointment. It will help heal the wound and prevent infection." He didn't look up as he spoke.

It was clear he knew what he was doing. When he was finished, he leaned back in the chair and glanced up at her. She moved her foot around and winced in pain.

"Like I said, it'll hurt for awhile, but you'll survive." He stood and held his hand out for her.

She glanced at it once before taking it and letting him help her off the bed. Before she could put any weight on the injured foot, Dorian scooped her off her feet and into his arms. Lalita was very aware that her breasts were perilously close to his mouth and that her bare pussy rubbed along the thick expanse of his forearm. Although there were all these temptations teasing him, Dorian kept his gaze forward as he led them back into the main entertainment room.

When they reached their destination, Lalita immediately noticed that all five men were present but seemed preoccupied with either conversation or video games. As if they sensed their presence, they all became quiet and turned and stared at the two of them.

"What the hell happened?" Aleck stood up so quickly that the controller he had in his lap tumbled to the ground.

"The vase in the East wing broke, and Lalita stepped on it." Dorian answered Aleck's question, but she was surprised to see his gaze on her.

"Fuck. Does this mean she's out of commission?" Silence descended over the room as all eyes stopped on Torryn. He looked around and knitted his brows when he noticed all attention was on him. "What?"

Lalita felt her face heat in embarrassment and struggled out of Dorian's grasp. Thankfully Dorian didn't object to her movement and set her on the ground. Torryn's comment stung, but she reminded herself she was here to do a job and he had every right to be pissed if she wasn't able to work.

"I'll be fine." Head kept toward the ground, Lalita was too mortified to look at any of them.

"Nice fucking attitude, asshole." Kane's voice sounded clipped and angry. Lalita chanced a glance at him and saw his back as he stormed out of the room.

"What a prick." She recognized Michael's terse words and watched as he stormed out of the room. She didn't miss how Michael's stare was on Torryn, a murderous glare in his eyes.

There was a collective murmur, and the rest of them left the room until it was only her and Dorian. As quiet as it had gone, she was sure crickets could have been heard chirping. Lalita refused to face Dorian and his anger over this situation as well.

"Lalita, look at me."

Obeying him was the first rule, and so she didn't hesitate in looking up at him. He wore a blank mask, as if everything that had just transpired hadn't affected him in the slightest. Hands in his pockets and stance easygoing, at the moment he didn't appear to be the brooding leader of five other men, but Lalita knew better.

"Torryn speaks out sometimes. I am not saying what he said was proper, but the best thing to do is ignore those comments."

Surprise flickered through her. She hadn't expected any kind of explanation in regards to what Torryn said, and she honestly didn't know how to take it. The only thing she could think to do was nod her head in agreement.

"Come here."

Not putting any weight on her foot, Lalita steadied herself on the back of the couch and moved toward him. She must have looked ridiculous trying to move because he took a couple of steps forward and wrapped his arm around her waist, bringing her body flush with his. The heat that he emitted was so strong her whole body felt alive. Need slammed into her, and her pussy became ready to take the hard cock he hid behind his slacks. She was so ready for him, so ready to be fucked and end the torment that had grown since their last encounter.

They stared at each other for so long Lalita started to become uncomfortable from the intensity of his eyes upon her. When he lifted his hand, she thought for sure he'd stroke her bare breast, but what he touched floored her. He stroked his big fingers down her cheek. It was a gentle caress, but it had her skin pebbling and a shiver skating down her spine. The touch was so soft and gentle that it went against everything she assumed Dorian to be. When she saw his head start to descend toward her, she knew her eyes had to look like saucers. Heart thumping madly, she was frozen as he brushed his lips against hers.

That first tentative touch seemed awkward, but when he added a little more pressure, she melted into him and accepted the kiss. The sound of their mouths moving together filled the room, seeming to make everything more erotic. The feel of his tongue stroking along the seam of her lips had her opening her mouth and meeting his gentle thrusts with her own. Tongues moving together in seductive motions,

Lalita pressed her belly more firmly into Dorian's straining erection. The long, thick rod jerked, as if the contact was too much.

Dorian's groan against her mouth ignited her own, and she pressed herself against the back of the couch. She needed to brace herself for the passionate kiss he was delivering. It was like he was a starved man and she was the first meal he had seen in ages. His hands were everywhere, stroking, tweaking, and rubbing every square inch of her body until she felt oversensitive. His deft fingers unlatched the corset she wore in a matter of seconds, and she let out a sigh against his mouth.

"Feel better?"

A nod was all she could accomplish, but thankfully that was an adequate answer for him, because he went back to kissing her. With the corset gone, her breasts swung lightly with every shift of their bodies. Lalita found herself getting pushed harder and harder against the couch as Dorian ground his cock into her belly.

When Dorian pulled back so that his lips barely skimmed hers, she wanted to lean forward and continue getting lost in his kiss, but his words stopped her.

"I want you so bad, Lalita." He took her hand and led it between their bodies and pressed it against his cock. "You'll give me what I want, won't you." It wasn't a question.

His shaft was rock hard and nearly throbbed against her palm. When he let go of her wrist, she kept her hand against him, feeling the heat of him through his trousers. She wanted him desperately. "I'll give you anything you want."

Chapter Five

Dorian's chuckle seemed to vibrate right down to her clit. "I know you will because you're such a good girl."

She would be a good girl, or a bad girl, or any other kind of girl he wanted, as long as he eased the ache in her pussy. When he stepped away from her, she was left feeling bereft and cold. Skin pebbled with sensitivity, Lalita wanted to go back to him, but when she pushed off the couch to do just that, a firm shake of his head stopped any and all of her movements.

"Get fully naked and sit on the loveseat with a leg over each armrest." They must really like to see her in that position, because it seemed like she was in it a great deal.

The heat Lalita felt from him just moments before seemed lost as he made his order clear. Getting naked right in front of him was easier said than done. She shouldn't have felt nervous around him, hell, she had sucked his cock just the other day.

When she was naked and placed the way he specified, she swallowed roughly. The way the loveseat was situated placed her back to Dorian. How she wished she could see his expression.

She sensed him before she actually saw him. When his fingers moved along her shoulder, she couldn't help but jump at the slight touch. It felt like fire on her skin and did nothing to help tame the raging inferno inside of her. He moved slowly around her until it seemed likes ages until he stood right in front of her. Lalita knew how her pussy looked, soaked, swollen, and red. Did the sight turn him on? Just seeing his eyes rake over her body was arousing the hell out of her.

"Touch yourself, Lalita. Take your fingers and spread those pretty red cunt lips so I can see what I'm about to devour."

Oh God. With trembling fingers she reached between her thighs and pulled her pussy lips apart. The sound of suctioning flesh pulling apart had her cheeks growing hot in embarrassment. The cream from her pussy slid down the crack of her ass, and when she chanced a look at Dorian, she saw that he was rubbing his dick through his trousers as he watched her.

"I'm going to suck on your pussy so good and hard you'll beg me to come, but I won't allow it until I'm buried deep inside of you." Words that sounded like a strangled groan left his lips right before he went to his knees between her splayed thighs.

He didn't wait for any more of an invitation than her pussy spread wide right in front of his face. He dove right in, dragging his tongue from her cunt hole to her clit. He did this over and over again until she could do nothing else but let her head fall back and her eyes slide shut.

He pushed her fingers out of the way and held her lips open for his tongue. When he slid it into her opening, she nearly came right then.

"If you come before I give you permission, I'll have to punish you." Dorian didn't even bother lifting his head to speak. He just mumbled the words against her saturated folds and continued to eat her out.

It seemed like hours before he finally allowed her a reprieve from his onslaught. It took all her willpower to hold in the pleas she wanted to shout at him, but she knew expressing them would only end up costing her more in the long run.

He ran his tongue up her slit once more before twirling his tongue around her clit and pushing away. It took all of her strength to peel her eyes open and stare at him. The feel of hot tears trekking down her cheeks wasn't nearly as startling as when he lifted his finger to brush them away. The act was so soothing she could have cried harder.

Her clit positively throbbed with the need for release. Her pussy felt swollen, and judging by the way Dorian's lips were red and shiny, she knew he had fucked her with his mouth so good that a simple wisp of air could get her off right now.

Compared to her breathing, Dorian's seemed calm and collected, but when she saw his hands go to his belt buckle, her breathing increased tenfold. The sound of metal clanking together and of a zipper sliding down seemed to drown out all other noises. Eyes riveted to what he was about to reveal, Lalita couldn't tear her gaze from the sight even if her life depended on it.

When he let his pants fall to the ground, she immediately saw that he wore no underwear. A thick and long cock sprang forth from a thatch of black hair. It looked like a beast, a third leg that could do some serious damage. Although she had seen the size of his cock the day before, Lalita was stunned anew when she saw it once again. Dorian's had certainly broken the mold. The head of his erection was flushed a deep red and shined from how the skin stretched over the thick crown.

How in the hell is that thing supposed to fit inside of me? True, she had given birth, but hell, that had been painful and something she didn't feel like experiencing again anytime soon. She was wet enough, she conceded, but still, he would have one hell of a time shoving that thing into her pussy.

Dorian unbuttoned his shirt and tossed it aside so that he now stood nude before her. His body was magnificent, all hard planes and dips in just the right places. He moved closer and bent back onto his knees until she felt the smooth skin of his erection slide against her vagina. A gasp welled up in her throat when he pushed his cock against her harder. The root nudged her clit, and tingles of electricity slammed into her.

"Come on in, boys."

Lalita froze with shock as soon as the words left Dorian's mouth. The sound of a door opening followed by several footsteps sounded behind her. Time seemed to stand still, and when she saw Kane, Torryn, Michael, Aleck, and Zakary take their places behind Dorian, everything became even more surreal. As if this had all been planned, which she now realized was very likely, they unbuckled their pants and let them fall to the floor. Lalita didn't know why she was stunned. This was what she signed up for, but she had never been an exhibitionist.

"Let us see how pretty her pussy looks, Dor." Kane spoke softly but with a rough edge.

Dorian leaned to the side. "Spread those pussy lips, baby. Make them wish it was them about to fuck you instead of me."

Lalita flicked her gaze to each man, and when she was greeted with hard stares, she quickly obliged. A few clearing of throats and muffled grunts sounded before Dorian moved back and shielded her pussy from the other five.

"Grab my cock and position it, Lalita."

Throat gone dry, she reached between them and gripped Dorian's hard flesh. His shaft felt like a hot poker in her hand, so warm she expected burn marks on her flesh. There was no trouble in aiming that monster cock at her opening, but instinctively she clenched around the bulbous head.

Dorian rested his hands on the armrests and hung his head. "Don't do things like that, or I won't last."

It wasn't as if she was doing it on purpose. Ever so slowly, Dorian started to push his way into her. The stretch and burn that the act initiated seemed to intensify the longer he was in her. As if her body wanted the intrusion out, her pussy involuntarily clenched and unclenched.

"Motherfucker." Breathing hard against her breasts, Dorian's words seemed strained and forced.

The more inches he shoved into her cunt, the more the pain blossomed into pleasure. When he finally stopped tunneling into her, he rested his forehead against her chest and breathed out harshly. Neither one of them moved for several moments. Lalita took that time to look at the five men watching them from beneath their lashes. They all had their cocks in their hands and were beating off with intent. All eyes were on her face, as if that alone was the sight that captivated them. They held her mesmerized for several long moments, but then when Dorian started to pull out of her she was brought back to the present.

When she lifted her hands to place them on his wide shoulders, his hands on her wrists stopped her movements. Dorian was quick as he placed her arms above her head and held them there with one hand. With his other hand now free, he pulled and tweaked one of her nipples until she was forced to bite her lip to stop the sound she would have made.

Dorian's movements were unhurried as he pulled his cock out of her and pushed it back in. Each time was like when he first entered her. There was the initial stretch and burn, and then those two sensations morphed into ecstasy. When she closed her eyes and finally moaned from the pleasure that coursed through her, Dorian's deep words had her breath stalling and any further noise ceasing from her mouth.

"Bring me the clamps."

Lalita opened her eyes and watched as Kane stepped out of his pants the rest of the way and moved over to a cabinet built into the wall. With Dorian's big body blocking her view, she couldn't get a clear view of what Kane was getting, that was, until he turned around and she saw what he held. Two alligator clips attached to a small box lay in his outstretched hand. Panic settled within her instantly.

Dorian let go of her wrists and cupped her cheek. He stared into her eyes for several seconds and then leaned in to kiss her. It wasn't a passionate kiss filled with heat, but more so a reassuring one that was meant to ease. At least that's the way she took it.

"Go on, Kane, attach them." Dorian spoke but kept his gaze on her. He moved back so that Kane had enough room to lean forward.

Lalita watched with a mixture of fear and anxiety as Kane took the two alligator clips and attached one to each nipple. There was no need for him to make the tips engorged, for they already stood out obscenely. When the clamps were firmly in place, Lalita could feel her heartbeat in each nipple. There was pain present from the blood flow being cut off, but that became a warmth that grew into a wildfire.

She stared at the beaded tips and watched in fascination as they turned a deep red and seemed to become even more swollen. Kane's blond hair suddenly blocked her view, and she gasped when she felt his tongue run across one distended tip. Because of the clamps, the buds were far more sensitive than she ever could have imagined.

When he lifted his head, he smiled and leaned in to run his tongue across her lips. It was strange being kissed by one man while another was buried in her pussy. She clenched around Dorian's cock and heard him growl.

In the next instant small volts of electricity coursed through each nipple. She arched her back from the intensity of it. Never had she felt anything so powerful before. It wasn't painful per se, but it sure as hell was a shock.

Off and on the electricity zinged through her nipples and right down to her clit. She could have sworn they had placed a clamp on the tender bud between her thighs if she didn't know any better. It was like her nipples and clit were one, and each time that current traveled through her tissue, it set off a domino effect of ecstasy.

Their beautiful torture seemed to last forever until she was finally begging them to let her come or to stop. Thankfully they were merciful Masters and unclamped the clips from her nipples, giving her a small reprieve to catch her breath.

"That's only a small taste of the things we have in store for you."

She didn't doubt Kane's words.

"Get the fuck out of here, Kane. You'll have your turn soon enough."

Kane moved back in line and immediately started running his hand over his swollen shaft. Dorian started to move inside of her, and Lalita closed her eyes and absorbed the pleasure and pain that morphed into one. Faster and faster he pumped, swiveling his hips so that he hit just the right spot to send her spiraling toward completion.

"Please, Master, please can I come?" Lalita peeled her eyes open and stared at him. Sweat beaded the wide, tanned expanse of his chest.

"How sweet it is to hear those words leave your mouth, but not yet, baby." As if those words had been a cue to the other five men, they all stepped closer and circled around her.

Harder and faster Dorian fucked her until she squeezed her hands so hard pain sprang to her palms. The noises surrounding her were harsh and real. Grunts, moans, and heavy panting filled the room, and she had to use every part of her strength to hold off from letting release take her away.

"Please, Dorian, oh God, please let me come. I can't hold it any longer." Her voice didn't sound like hers. It was breathy and heavy, like a woman that was right on the verge.

"All right, baby, come all over my cock." Just like that, his command and permission set off a series of small orgasms inside of her that exploded into one giant cataclysm.

It had seemed like forever of wanting this exact moment. So long she had been teased. Back arched and breasts thrust forward, Lalita couldn't help the screams of pleasure that left her. She felt Dorian's own release inside of her. He came long and hard until his cum slipped down the crack of her ass. Whether he made any noise of pleasure or not was lost to her. She was too wrapped up in her own ecstasy to pay much attention to anything going on around her. When she thought the pleasure was over, Dorian wrapped his arms around her waist and lifted her off the loveseat. He was on his back and had her draped over his body without even coming undone from her body. His cock was still hard inside of her and every time her pussy clenched around the hardened flesh he groaned.

With Dorian still buried in her cunt, she sensed someone moving behind her. A quick glance over her shoulder proved that Aleck was taking his place, cock in hand.

"Relax, baby. I promise to make this feel really good for you." Aleck's words were filled with sexual promise and dark eroticism.

Never had she been fucked in the ass, and the idea frightened her.

"Look at me, Lalita." Dorian cupped her chin and lifted her head so they were staring in each other's eyes again. "No one will hurt you. I promise." Bringing her face closer to his, he kissed her deeply. The kiss was sensual and had her arousal climbing to the surface again, but it didn't deter her from the fact that Aleck was about to shove his huge cock in her ass.

Warm liquid sliding between the cheeks of her ass startled her, but Dorian kept his lips firmly on hers and intensified the kiss. Aleck rubbed the lube around her anus and then slipped the digit inside. First one finger and then two were inserted. He scissored his fingers in her body, stretching her, preparing her for what was about to come. When Aleck positioned the tip of his shaft at her anus, her whole body tensed. Aleck ran his hands over the mounds of her ass and whispered words that she knew where meant to soothe. They knew this was her first time having anal sex, and she was thankful they understood that this was a frightening time for her.

With Dorian still hard and buried in her cunt, Aleck pushed the head of his cock into her ass. The feel of muscles burning was intense. The tip of his shaft finally popped through the tight ring of muscle and he slowly slid into her. Never had she felt this full. When Aleck's abdomen was pressed against her ass Dorian finally broke the kiss. She breathed out deeply, never knowing that she would feel so filled having two cocks in her at one time.

As if having a mind of its own, her pussy clenched, which in turn had her ass clenching around Aleck as well. Both men groaned, but that wasn't the only sound that filled the room. Skin slapping against skin, fast and heavy breathing, and grunts were a hearty combination in the room. Curiosity getting the better of her, Lalita looked over her shoulder at the other four men. Their hands were like blurs of speed as they stroked their dicks and watched her. Sweat was pooled across their foreheads and down the rippling muscles of their chests.

"Look at me. Lalita." She turned her head and looked at Dorian. He gripped her waist and started to slowly pull out of her. The position they were in made it so he couldn't fully leave her body, but it still took a skill she was unaccustomed to.

When he was as far out of her body as he could get, he pushed back into her. Biting her lip because it felt so good, she felt Aleck start to pull out of her ass. It was a strange feeling, having one man push into her pussy while another pulled out of her ass. When the tip of Aleck's dick was almost all the way out he pushed back into her. The two of them rotated their movements slowly at first, but with each passing moment they increased their momentum until she was forced to hold on as her body was jarred between the two of them.

Faster and harder they pushed into her. Her skin was slick with perspiration and rubbed between the two of them. The pain and pleasure of having two men filling her at once had her biting her lip so hard she tasted blood. She forced her eyes to remain open and couldn't help but glance at Zakary, Michael, Torryn, and Kane while she got fucked. As if she had spoken with her eyes, Torryn stepped in front of her and pressed his shaft against her mouth. She greedily opened and ran her tongue along the bulbous head. He tasted salty and earthy. It was a heady combination.

He fucked her mouth with hard, quick thrust. Small jets of cum spilled from him, but before he fully ejaculated in her mouth he pulled away and Kane stepped forward. She eagerly sucked on Kane's dick. She pressed her tongue into the slit at the tip, wanting to taste a mouthful of cum, but was disappointed when he pulled away all too soon. When Zakary stepped forward, she was already on the verge of climaxing herself and was frantic for his cock in her mouth.

"Easy, baby." Zakary had an almost pained look on his face as she gripped his shaft and stroked it as she sucked on the tip. God she wanted to taste him. Just like the two before him, when he was just about to ejaculate he pulled away from her.

When Michael stepped in front of her, he ran the pad of his thumb over her bottom lip. As if she wasn't herself, she opened her mouth and sucked the digit inside. Using her teeth, she gently bit his thumb while staring into his eyes. Michael's breathing was just as accelerated as Dorian and Aleck's, and when he pulled his finger out of her mouth and replaced it with his dick, she groaned loudly. At that point it didn't matter because she was so lost in pleasure she couldn't think straight.

"Tell us you want our cum filling you up, baby." Aleck's words were whispered and heated by her ear.

Michael pulled his cock out of her mouth all too soon. "I do. I want it so bad." She was panting so hard that the words came out as small breaths. She knew they heard her nonetheless. The sound of skin slapping against skin and of her breasts jiggling and rubbing against Dorian's equally slick chest had her orgasm tearing forth. "Oh God. I'm going to come."

"Do it baby. Come all over my cock."

A long groan left her and a second later she heard Dorian and Aleck make the same sound. Hot cum filled her cunt and ass, and she wanted more. Falling forward on Dorian's chest because she couldn't hold herself up any longer, she panted for breath. As the minutes went by, both men remained buried inside of her. Aleck was the first to pull out and gripped her around the waist. She had no idea what he was doing, but when Dorian pulled out of her as well and got off the couch, she knew it wasn't over yet.

Aleck set her back on the couch and she gratefully laid back on it. Legs still spread wide, she stared at the four men that had yet to get off. Kane, Michael, Torryn, and Zakary moved closer until they surrounded her. They pumped their fists over their cocks maddeningly, each of their faces awash with ecstasy.

"Ask them for their cum, Lalita." Dorian's voice sounded from somewhere in the room, but she kept her attention on the other men.

Despite the fact she had just gotten off hard, something inside of her wanted these men to come all over her, to cover her body with their spunk. "Please, please come all over me." She meant it, too.

"Touch yourself." Torryn's voice was strained. He stood between her legs, his eyes riveted to what she knew was a swollen, cum-covered pussy.

Lalita reached between her thighs, her cunt so sensitive she winced when her fingers brushed across the folds. She plucked at her clit, first running small circles around it and then picking up speed and rubbing harder and faster. She could feel semen slipping out of her body and coating her labia. She used it as lubrication to pleasure herself for them. She didn't think she could have came again after the orgasm she just had, but as she watched these men jerk off in front of her, she was perilously close to another climax.

Four sets of eyes were on what she was doing now. Their bodies glistened with sweat, their hands nothing more than blurs of speed over their shafts. Her orgasm raced to the surface when she heard the first man utter a feral growl. As if on cue, all four men groaned in unison. Arcs of hot, white cum shot out of the tips of their dicks and splashed on her body. The feel of that warm liquid on every part of her drew her orgasm to the top, and she threw her head back, closed her eyes, and moaned aloud. Breasts, belly, neck, and even her legs were covered with their seed.

The only thing that could be heard was the heavy panting of several bodies in the room. When Lalita could finally pry her eyes open, she noticed that all the men were staring at her as if they didn't quite know what to make of her. Strange looks covered their faces, but when they noticed she was watching them just as intently, they turned their attentions elsewhere.

Each one cleaned himself off and got dressed before leaving the room, not even a word uttered. Uncomfortable silence filled the room as she saw Dorian leaning against the fireplace watching her. He was already dressed and held a large rag in his hand. He pushed off the mantle and walked toward her. She didn't know what to expect, but it certainly wasn't what he did next.

He gently cleaned between her tender thighs. She took the rag from him and smiled gratefully and cleaned the rest of her body off. What she needed was a nice hot bath to sooth her sore muscles and aching body.

Dorian held his hand out and helped her off the couch. "Come on, I think that deserves a hot bath." Despite the intimate encounter they had just shared, his voice sounded void of any emotions. It didn't even matter at the moment, because the idea of a hot bath was forefront in her mind.

Chapter Six

Lalita sat back and watched as Dorian filled the bathtub with water. A generous portion of bubble bath had been applied and threatened to spill over the side.

"I'll leave you to soak. Don't take too long because I'm sure you'll have visitors."

Dorian left the bathroom and shut the door behind him with a soft click. Lalita was confused by his statement. She honestly didn't think her pussy could handle any more sex right now, but per the contract, she wasn't supposed to deny any of them.

Blowing out a deep breath, she slipped into the tub and sighed out in bliss. The hot, bubbly water instantly soothed her sore muscles and tender pussy. Bottles with foreign labels lined the edge of the tub, and Lalita grabbed one and popped the lid. The scent of jasmine and honey filled the room. She washed her hair and the rest of her body with the heavenly scented soap. When she was as clean as she was going to get, she slipped further into the tub and rested her head on the back of it.

The feeling of being weightless further relaxed her, and she smiled, wishing this moment would never end. She had no qualms about pleasing the six men, but they were insatiable, and she was no spring chicken. She certainly wasn't going to ask them to go easy on her and risk them getting ideas in their heads.

With her eyes closed and her mind drifting, Lalita let her arms float beside her and the bubbles coast over her breasts. She could stay in the warm water forever, just letting all the troubles of her life wash away and go down the drain.

She opened her eyes sometime later, the water now lukewarm and her skin pruned. Goose bumps popped out along her skin when she got out of the tub and wrapped a towel around her body. Lalita looked at herself in the mirror. There were dark circles around her eyes, and her hair was a mess. The bath had relaxed her initially, but now she felt sore and exhausted. What she needed was to get a good night's rest.

A squeak of surprise left her when she opened the bathroom door and saw Zakary standing on the other side, with a grin on his face.

Taking her hand, he led her out of the bathroom and back into her room. She expected to see the rest of the men lying in wait for her, but the room was empty.

"Tonight is my night."

"Your night?"

Zakary's smile widened, and he sat on the bed. "Not scared are you?"

This teasing note from him seemed strange. True, she didn't know him at all, but from her first impression of him, he had seemed more standoffish. Now, though, Zakary had a devilish grin on his face and eyed her body like it was a piece of candy and he was a kid going through sugar withdrawal.

Whether he wanted her to actually answer him was a mystery to her because when she didn't utter a word, he leaned back on the bed, propped his hands behind his head, and told her exactly what he wanted from her.

"Drop the towel, turn around, and grab your ankles."

Holy. Fucking. Shit.

Lalita didn't move right away, but when she saw his mischievous grin start to turn into a frown, she quickly jumped into action. When her hands were wrapped around her ankles, she closed her eyes and willed herself to calm down. She was still sore from her earlier romp with Dorian and Aleck.

"Spread your thighs wider. I want to see *my* pussy."

The way he emphasized "*my* pussy" startled her. It was like that particular anatomy was a piece of property, his property.

The sound of the bed squeaking as Zakary got off of it had Lalita's heart thumping madly. For several long moments nothing was said. She could feel his body heat directly behind her, knew that he was staring right at her vagina, and wondered if he liked what he saw. The position she held was starting to become increasingly uncomfortable, but before she could utter a complaint, a hot, wet mouth suctioned between her thighs.

A small cry left her lips as Zakary spread her labia apart and licked at her center. He was ruthless and demanding, never relenting as he shoved his tongue deep into her pussy.

"I'm not going to make you suffer, sweetling. You'll find me much more giving than Dorian."

His words were lost on her. She was far too gone from the feeling of his mouth moving over her vagina, of his tongue stroking not only her pussy hole but also her clit. The soreness started to dissipate as ecstasy took its place.

Zakary unlatched his mouth from her and covered her back with his chest. "Tell me you want my cock shoved so far up your cunt you can't even see straight."

She swallowed when his shaft pressed against her wet folds. She hadn't heard him remove his clothes, but he was certainly nude, if all that warm, hard flesh was anything to go by. He ran his hands over her belly and up to cup her breasts.

"I want your cock so far up me I can't see straight."

"That's what I wanted to hear." He all but purred the words against her flesh before he licked a path over the back of her neck and bit the side of her throat. Not letting his hold on her loosen, he walked them backward. He was skilled as he moved them in sync and tweaked her nipples all at the same time. When he stopped, he spun her around and placed his hand in the middle of her back.

"Grip the sheets, Lalita. You're going to need to hold on for what I'm about to do."

His words were like lava straight to every erogenous zone on her body. He was so demanding that she didn't even dare disobey. When she had a fistful of sheets between her hands, she felt him nudge her legs apart wider. He ran his finger up and down her cleft slowly at first and then picked up speed. Maybe the hot bath had loosened her up more than she had realized and that was why she was ready for another go-round?

His hot breath wafted right by her ear a second before he whispered, "Soon I'm going to fuck this tight little ass of yours." She bit her lip when his finger ran across her anus. "Not tonight, though. Tonight I'm going to have you coming all over my cock."

He pressed her on the bed firmer with his hand on her back. She could feel him run his erection up and down her slit, lubing himself up for when he impaled her. Without any more talk, Zakary pressed the tip of his shaft at her pussy and thrust forward so hard that she slid up the bed.

Breath literally knocked out of her, Lalita could do nothing else but hold on tight as Zakary fucked her so hard and fast everything was a blur.

"Come for me, Lalita."

As if his words were an aphrodisiac, a fierce orgasm started at her toes and made its way up her spine. Like a firecracker, it exploded out of her so harshly that she couldn't contain the loud cry of pleasure that came from her.

"That's it. Make my cock all slick with your juices." He thrust harder and faster in her. The sound of wet, sloppy sex rang throughout the room. It somehow made the act dirty yet tantalizing all in the same breath.

His hands landed on her ass cheeks so hard that she immediately felt the blood rush to the surface. Over and over he slapped her ass, growling obscenities and panting heavily. He gripped the now-tender mounds and pulled them apart until she felt the air brush across her puckered rear hole.

Before Zakary got off he pulled out of her, flipped her onto her back, and speared his dick back into her once again. He felt different from Dorian and Aleck, not as long or thick, but still with an impressive girth that left her dazed. "Hold onto the headboard and don't let go." Deep, dominating words held no argument.

When she reached back but only touched air, he gripped her hips and pushed her up the bed without taking his cock out of her. The wrought iron bars chilled her hands when she finally curled her fingers around them, but it was a welcome sensation on her overheated flesh.

"You feel so fucking good. So tight, hot, and wet."

Oh yes, it certainly felt good.

"Whose cock is making this pussy all creamy?"

The dirty talk was definitely something new to her. With Brad it had been pretty vanilla sex, but she admitted that hearing what Zakary had to say drove her arousal so high she didn't think it would ever come back down.

"Your cock is making me all wet."

"That's fucking right, baby." Sweat dripped down his chest, and she had the urge to trace her tongue along the path. "So. Fucking. Good." He slammed into her once more before stilling and letting out a feral groan.

Never once did he take his eyes off of her, and she felt every tremor of his cock when it jerked inside of her as he emptied his cum into her body. Although she had come just moments before, her pussy still quivered with tiny pleasure-filled aftershocks. As if he had no more strength left, Zakary collapsed on top of her. His weight was stupendous, and she gasped for air. Thankfully he sensed her distress and rolled off of her.

Cramps settled into her arms from hanging onto the headboard. When she turned to look at him, she noticed he watched her.

"I'm sorry, sweetling." She was confused as to what he was talking about until he lifted his hands above her head and pried her fingers off the poles. "I shouldn't have made you hold on so long. Your poor fingers are probably sore." He rubbed the kinks out of her fingers and arms.

"I'm okay, more than okay, really." It seemed like the right thing to say at the moment.

Zakary held a purely satisfied male grin on his lips. "You sure know how to make a guy feel good." Arms stretched above his head, Lalita couldn't help but admire his physique. "Well, it's been fun, but I'll let you get some sleep."

He was off the bed and dressed so quickly all she could do was stare at him in shock. When he had said it was his night, she had assumed he would be spending the *entire* night with her. Apparently their versions were vastly different. She shouldn't complain, though. A good night's sleep alone would do her mind and body good.

He left her alone in the darkened room, naked, his cum slipping out from between her thighs. *Way to make a girl feel special.*

* * * *

After Zakary left, although she was exhausted, she found herself lying wide awake in the middle of the night. When she glanced at the clock, she saw it was three in the morning. Sleep was obviously not an option at the moment. As if her stomach agreed with her, it gave a mighty growl. The dinner she had eaten hours ago hadn't been anything substantial. Of course that had been her fault. She had been so nervous to really eat anything that she had picked over her food instead of actually ingesting it.

The smart thing to do would have been to stay in bed and try to get some rest. Heaven knew tomorrow was probably going to be even more exhausting then the day before. Her stomach won out in the end, though.

Whole body sore from earlier activities, Lalita winced as she finally stood. Still nude, she grabbed a long T-shirt from her bag and slipped it on. It fell to her thighs, which normally she would have felt too exposed, but given the things she was required to wear here, made her feel overdressed.

The house was silent and still as she made her way down the stairs and into the kitchen. She didn't dare turn on a light and risk waking the rest of the house, so she grabbed a few items out of the fridge and sat at the island. The silence descended around her as well as the darkness. Right as she brought her last forkful of apple pie to her mouth, she heard heavy footfalls making their way down the stairs.

Fork halfway to her mouth, Lalita set it gently down on the plate. A large shadowed form stepped inside and froze as he no doubt saw her sitting there. She couldn't make out who it was right away, but when they stepped fully inside and the moonlight slashed across his features, her heart instantly sped up. Michael only wore a pair of drawstring pants and nothing else. The pants hung low on his hips, and a striking V on his lower abdomen made her heart palpitate.

He was void of any hair on his chest, but a dark line of hair made a path starting below his belly button and disappeared beneath his pants. A warm gush of moisture slipped out of Lalita's pussy as she saw the raw masculinity standing before her.

Michael's dark hair was disheveled, but the sight only made her hotter. Everything from his sleep-filled look, to his bulging biceps, to the impressively defined chest reeked raw power and male pheromones. Mouth now dry and pie forgotten, Lalita found herself getting out of the chair. Her inner thighs were starting to get moist from her juices, but she didn't care. She wanted all her cream spread along his cock as he pounded away inside of her.

Neither of them said anything as they slowly moved toward one another. The closer he got to her, Lalita could see the erection that strained against his pants. Oh yes, he wanted exactly what she did as well. When they were an inch from each other, he reached up and cupped the side of her cheek. He didn't wait any longer. He leaned down and brought his lips to hers for a scorching kiss that had her toes curling.

Not thinking clearly at that point, Lalita wrapped her arms around his biceps. She dug her nails into his warm, smooth flesh and moved closer to him. Her breasts pressed against his chest, and her nipples instantly stabbed out. Head tilted for better access to his mouth, Lalita kissed him like she was dying. He wrapped his arms around her body and started moving them backward until she felt the counter hit her back.

As if that was his cue, he became a wild man. The shirt was torn from her body. The sound of fabric being rendered useless seemed extraordinarily loud in the kitchen, but she was far too gone to care. His pants were next to go until there was nothing standing between them. He gripped her ass and lifted her onto the counter. Lalita wrapped her thighs around his waist and used her heels to pull him closer. His cock, hot, hard, and thick, nudged at her cunt. The fact that neither of them uttered a word seemed to make the situation even more intense.

Without wasting another minute, Michael grabbed his cock and placed the tip at her entrance. He thrust into her hard and fast, and she gasped at the feeling. With their kiss now broken, Lalita closed her eyes and let her head fall back as he pounded into her. The sound of her pussy sucking at his dick had her climax rushing to the surface. Maybe she should have said she was about to come, but she couldn't have found her voice at that moment anyway.

He gently lowered her to the counter while never missing a beat. The tile was freezing compared to her overheated body. His hands were so big they seemed to span her entire waist as he fucked her. Thrusts long and deep, Michael was ruthless as he stared down at her with heavy-lidded eyes. Mouth open because she couldn't seem to suck in enough oxygen, Lalita let her orgasm wash through her. As if he knew what was happening, he pumped into her once more and stilled. He didn't utter a word, not even a groan of satisfaction.

Lalita might have been worried he hadn't enjoyed it if not for the way the muscles in his body were corded tight and a look of pure ecstasy that crossed his features. When they were both sated, he helped her into a sitting position and wrapped his arms around her. She wasn't cold, but she started to shiver nonetheless. They stayed like that for so long that Lalita started to grow drowsy. She couldn't explain it, but at that moment she felt a spark of something more. Maybe it was a ridiculous notion given her situation, but she felt like a woman.

Chapter Seven

"I don't think my pussy can take any more sex." Lalita stared at herself in the mirror. Several weeks had already passed, and she didn't think one body could handle so much sex. The men were insatiable with their appetites, and she was starting to notice their personalities were very different. She was also starting to see a pattern with their attentions to her. For several days straight one man would stay with her, and then they would switch off with another man. It was confusing at times because she was increasingly exhausted from their attentions and there were times the days seemed to mesh into one.

Tonight was Aleck's night. He appeared to be the youngest of the group and, before he had fucked her ass, the gentlest of the six of them. Although she was excited to be with all the men, she was especially excited to see what kind of lover Aleck would be. Even though she had been with everyone intimately, she had yet to see Aleck again.

She looked at herself once more in the mirror. Apparently there were going to be no other men present for Aleck's time with her, which she admitted was a bit strange. She had grown used to all of them being around when she got fucked or performed other "duties" they deemed her responsibility. A candlelit dinner for two in the garden was Aleck's idea of starting the night off right, and she was all for a little quiet time.

He had picked out the dress for her to wear. It was a white strapless chiffon dress that hung loosely down her body and brushed the floor. It certainly wasn't like any of the other costumes the others had chosen for her. For one thing, the gown actually covered her pussy and breasts. During her time at the estate she had worn little to nothing, so being fully dressed seemed almost out of place.

One last look at herself in the mirror and she was ready to meet Aleck. When she reached the top landing, she saw him standing at the bottom of the stairs, tux and all. He looked so young.

When she reached the bottom, the look on his face had her nerves coming alive. "Wow, you look absolutely stunning."

A fierce heat spread up her neck and covered her face. She had never been very good with compliments. "Thank you."

He held the crook of his arm out to her, and she accepted. They walked side by side out the French doors and into the warm night. Weeks had passed, yet she had never ventured into the garden. Hell, she hadn't really left the bedroom.

It was a magnificent sight. Everything was manicured to perfection, and night-blooming flowers were placed intricately in flowerbeds. A small two-person table was situated under an arch of climbing vines. Twinkling lights illuminated the garden and created an ethereal glow that made everything seem like a dream.

"It's so beautiful." She probably sounded like a child.

Aleck led them over to the table and held her chair out for her. When she sat and he pushed it in, she could feel the brush of his silky hair along the back of her neck.

"It doesn't compare to your beauty, though."

The nervousness she felt was like being on a first date, which in all honesty was ridiculous given the fact he had fucked her ass just a few short weeks ago. Aside from that one dominating encounter, Aleck was always a gentleman. The way she was starting to feel for these men bordered on dangerous. She reminded herself that this was all part of the game. They had hired her to do a job, and it wouldn't do any good to let herself feel something more than what was actually there. She knew she needed to snap out of that before it got her in trouble.

Their meal was already laid out on the table in covered dishes, but she highly doubted any of the men had prepared it themselves. During her time at the estate, their meals had consisted of takeout or food that had already been prepared and then frozen.

They ate in virtual silence, but Lalita was very aware of how Aleck kept looking at her. The way he watched her didn't seem gentle or shy in the least. It was more of a look a lion gave its prey before it pounced.

When their meal came to an end Aleck helped her out of her seat and wrapped his arms around her. Lips pressed against hers, she got lost in the feel of his soft yet strong mouth on hers. He was a hesitant kisser at first, barely brushing his tongue against hers. He planted his hands firmly on her lower back and brought her closer to him until their bodies were flush. The kiss was soft, but it woke up her desire quickly.

Although there was no music playing, their bodies started to sway slightly as the kiss finally deepened. Aleck was definitely aroused, if the stiff erection pressed against her belly was anything to go by, but he seemed to want to take things slow. She didn't mind going easy, but his attentions toward her were so different from the other men's or the way he had behaved toward her just a few short weeks ago. Whereas the other five made no secret about what they wanted or how they wanted it, Aleck was becoming more of a mystery that she was finding she wanted to solve most urgently.

As if the imaginary song ended, Aleck broke the kiss and stared into her eyes. There was a sensation that passed through her that she couldn't describe. Warmth bloomed within her and encompassed her entire body, reminding her of that warm, relaxing bath she had taken where she felt safe and protected.

He took her hand and led them out of the garden and up the stairs. Neither of them spoke, but it was a comfortable silence. When they reached the landing, she expected him to lead her to her room, as did all the other men, but he surprised her by taking her down the opposite corridor and down a long, dimly lit hallway.

When they stopped at the last door on the left, he pulled a key out of his pocket and unlocked it. Lalita's palms started to sweat at the thought of what was behind a door he needed to lock.

"It's just us tonight?" She knew the answer to her question already, and even if she didn't, she couldn't have stopped the words from coming forth anyway. Aleck didn't answer her. Instead, he smiled a grin that couldn't be called anything but wicked and pushed the door open.

Dress bunched in her hands, Lalita stared into the pitch-black room. A gentle nudge from Aleck had her taking a few steps inside. She could hear her rapid breathing in the darkened room, and if she hadn't been able to feel Aleck's warm body right behind her, she would have felt all alone, as if a hole had swallowed her.

There wasn't nearly enough light from the hallway to show her what the room hid, and when Aleck shut the door, she was covered in a blanket of darkness.

"Aleck?"

"Shhh," he whispered by her ear. She felt him run his finger down the exposed skin of her back and shivered. "You aren't afraid of the dark, are you, little Lalita?"

No longer did Aleck sound unsure and hesitant. He sounded like a man that was playing a game, one that knew exactly what he was doing and got off on it.

"Answer me, Lalita."

"Yes." She didn't know why she had answered that truthfully. She should have lied. It was never good to reveal a weakness.

"I have a secret." He wasn't behind her any longer. She couldn't pinpoint his voice exactly because it seemed to echo throughout the whole room.

"You do?" Heart beating so hard she felt it in her throat, Lalita didn't dare move. Although she couldn't see a thing, she had a feeling Aleck could see her perfectly.

"I do. You see, my tastes aren't like the others." A light flickered on to showcase a large bed in the center of the room.

It was the size of the bed and the contraptions that were on the bed that had her heart stopping. Ropes were tied to the four corners of the posts, long enough to restrain someone if need be. A swing-type apparatus hung from glistening steel bolts attached to the ceiling. It didn't look like any swing she had ever seen, not with all the leather straps, handcuffs, and other clip-like appendages hanging off of it.

If that wasn't enough, another light to her left went on to showcase a long table filled with dildos of every shape and size, ball gags, and metal poles with straps attached to them, and an array of other things she wasn't even going to try and distinguish added to the mystery of it.

She instinctively looked to the right, which was still shrouded in darkness. As if he had been waiting for her to do just that, the light turned on to show an X-shaped board. Thick-looking straps were secured at each corner of the table, giving it an almost-ominous appearance.

"You see, sweet Lalita, my taste runs a little darker than my associates."

What in the hell is going on here? She supposed the saying about it always being the quiet ones was dead on with Aleck. This whole time she thought him quiet and the gentlest of the six despite the anal sex they had. It was clear he was the most dominating.

The dress she wore seemed grossly innocent for the occasion, and she glanced down at it. The material was butter soft, nothing compared to the leather and stainless steel that was housed in this room.

As if he read her mind, Aleck stepped out of the darkness and spoke. "I always did like the analogy about the innocent lamb being offered up to the wolf." No longer did he wear the tux that made him look so handsome. He now wore black leather pants and no shirt. He wasn't as muscular as the other five, but more like a lean swimmer, all toned sinew and tendons.

"Come here, my little lamb."

This might be a little too much for her, but she wasn't about to back down now, not when she had already come this far. That first step seemed like the hardest. When she was in front of him, she realized her hands shook uncontrollably. Clasping them in front of her, she saw Aleck glance down.

"You have no reason to be frightened, Lalita. Was I not gentle with you before? I tried not to take control, but sometimes when something as beautiful as you is presented, the temptation is too much to resist." He ran his finger down her cheek. "This is all part of the game you signed up for." He took her hands into his and brought them to his mouth for a kiss. "I'll tell you what. If at any time you feel so frightened that you want to stop, all you have to say is the safe word. I promise not to tell the others or hold it against you."

He didn't elaborate on what the safe word was, and she had a sneaking suspicion he wanted her to ask him herself.

After a hesitated moment she asked, "What's the safe word?" His smile proved she had been right.

He dropped her hands and circled her body. Lalita didn't move, didn't even lift her head to watch him. "Innocence. Yes, that seems like a fitting word for you." When he was in front of her again, he eyed her up and down and told her to strip.

The clasp to the dress was on the side, so she had no trouble slipping out of the gown. Per his instructions, she hadn't worn any panties or a bra, so when the material fell to the floor, she was left completely nude in front of him. Aleck circled her again, and this time she felt his hands smooth over her ass.

"Mmm, this ass looks tempting, but tonight I have other plans." His chest now pressed against her back, he pushed his hard cock against the crease of her ass. "Was this pretty little ass a virgin before I took it?"

He acted like he didn't know every personal, sexually oriented detail about her life. She hadn't lied about having previously been married or having a child. She hadn't denied only being with one person or never having anal sex. Aleck just wanted to hear it.

"You are the only man that has ever fucked me in the ass."

A tsking noise came from him before he frowned. "Now, now, Lalita. Ladies aren't supposed to speak like that. Why don't you say it the way you know you should say it?"

So this is how he wanted to play it. She was supposed to be the innocent submissive and him the dominating Master.

"Before you, no one has ever taken me back there, Sir."

"I like how you call me Sir, but I think I'd like to hear my name fall from your lips from now on. Is that understood?"

"Yes, Aleck." His voice was rougher. She could tell by the tone of it that she would either obey him and play by his rules, or she would be punished.

"Come with me, Lalita." Taking her hand in his, he led them over to the table. She felt her eyes widen at the assortment of sexual paraphernalia littered on the red velvet background. "You see these anal plugs, love? I want you to choose one."

By the look in his eyes, she knew he was dead serious. She eyed the ten or so anal plugs laid out before her. They all ranged from biggest to smallest, and she finally decided on one.

"I knew you'd pick the smallest one." He plucked it out of her hand and set it back on the table. His fingers skimmed over each one and then back again before stopping on a big, thick clear one with straps hanging from it.

Hell no. That thing was easily as thick as their cocks, if not larger.

"That won't fit." She looked at him with an expression she knew was a deer-in-the-headlights look.

He stared back at her, but his expression stayed stoic. The anal plug plunked down on the table with a loud thud. Aleck turned toward her and shook his head. "I thought you knew the rules. I didn't give you permission to speak. I was only jesting about big boy there"—he pointed to the anal plug he had just set down—"but because you spoke out of line, I think you need to be punished."

Chapter Eight

Aleck picked up the "big boy" as well as a bottle of lube. "Be a good girl and don't look so scared. I promise I'll make it good for you." He took her hand and led her over to the bed. "Turn around and bend so your belly is flush with the mattress."

This was like a nightmare. Lalita could not believe this was about to happen. How in the hell was he supposed to fit that thing up her ass? Forget about the uncomfortable aspect of it, the size alone was far bigger than any of the men and was enough to have her insides quiver. Time seemed to slow to a standstill. It seemed like forever before she felt the gentle glide of his lube-slicked finger run across her anus.

When he pressed the tip of the bottle into her ass and gave it a good squeeze, she could feel her eyes widen. The chill from the lube startled her, but not as much as the thought that he was lubing her up so thoroughly because he needed to fit that monster inside of her.

He removed the bottle and ran his finger over the tight bud once more. His body heat penetrated the skin of her back, and she knew he was right above her. A leather-clad erection pressed against her thigh, and then he ran his tongue across the shell of her ear.

He placed the tip of the plug against her anus. "Bear down and accept your punishment." Ever so slowly he pushed it into her ass. Pain was inevitable, but the feeling of being completely full overrode even that.

Sweat blossomed along her brow as she bore down and accepted it. An uncomfortable feeling settled within her when the plug was fully embedded in her ass. Lalita let out a breath she hadn't realized she had been holding and closed her eyes. She could feel straps being secured around her waist and each thigh. She glanced down and saw that the straps that had hung from the plug were there for more than just decoration. They were to secure it inside of her so she wouldn't be able to push it out.

Aleck stepped back and took his body heat with him. "Now stand up and let me see how pretty you look."

The very idea of standing with that thing rammed up her ass did not sound like a very good idea at all. *It's either do as he says or face another one of his "punishments."*

Her random thought had her slowly rising. A groan of discomfort almost spilled out of her mouth when she finally stood as erect as she could. Lips clamped tight, Lalita knew making any kind of noise would not be tolerated. With the anal plug in her ass, she couldn't even stand up straight, not comfortably at least.

"Come here, sweetling."

Moving toward him was a little easier said than done. When she stood right in front of him, he lifted his hand and skimmed his fingers over a distended nipple. A shiver raced up her body at the light touch. Aleck held her gaze and leaned in to brush his lips across hers.

"I think we're going to have a lot of fun tonight, Lalita." The words were murmured against her mouth seductively, sensually.

She could smell and taste the red wine he had drank at dinner, and it seemed to inflame her senses. With their lips pressed together again, Lalita let herself fall into the gentle caress of Aleck's mouth on hers. Just as she was letting herself fall into it, a slice of pain brought her back to the present. Aleck had her nipple between his thumb and forefinger and pinched it roughly.

"I want you in the middle of the bed, arms and legs spread wide." Just like that, he said what he wanted to and moved back to the table.

She stared at his back for a second and went over to the bed. Moving onto it and getting into the position he specified was a little more difficult than she thought it would be. For one thing, the anal plug made her movements stiff and uncomfortable. When she was sprawled out in the middle of the bed, she turned to look at him. His back still to her, he was picking up items off the table. When he finally turned back around, he wore a wicked grin that had her stomach dropping.

"You see the restraints on the posts?"

Lalita looked at each of the four posts that he pointed out and saw the straps he spoke of. Although she had never done anything related to bondage, she wasn't naive. There had been plenty of movies she had seen that touched on the aspect of being tied up and spanked, but as she looked at Aleck, she knew it wouldn't be that cut-and-dry.

"Have you ever been restrained?" He walked over to her and laid the items he picked off the table onto the bed. There were things she had never seen but she sure as hell could guess what they were for. A handle was attached to numerous thin leather straps. That one was easier enough to discern as a whip, but that wasn't the only one he had brought with him. Another one that resembled a paddle was covered in thick silver studs. Her ass clenched involuntarily at the thought of that coming into contact with her flesh.

When she saw the ball gag, her throat went dry. There were several clamps, a blindfold, a wicked looking dildo, and something that looked like a steel pipe with bands on each end.

"Wouldn't it be fun to use all of these tonight? Some of these items must look strange to you." Aleck ran his hand over each one.

It wasn't stated as a question, so she didn't answer.

"I knew you were the perfect female when you first walked into the room." She had wondered why they had picked her. Surely there had been prettier and more experienced woman that had applied. "The others were too fake and transparent. Not you, though. When you walked in, I swear I could see your heart start to race through your chest. You looked like you had just walked in to a house full of ravenous wolves." He sat on the edge of the bed and ran his finger up her leg. "I guess, in a way, you did." He met her gaze and smiled.

"That's why we picked you, Lalita. You were filled with truth and innocence."

He picked up the dildo and held it up for her to see. There seemed to be beads at the tip of the shaft. It was long and thick and the base had what appeared to be some kind of control panel on it. She was wet, but was she wet enough to take something like that into her body?

A click sounded, and Lalita felt her eyes widen in surprise. The beads at the head of the dildo started to move in a circular motion. Another click sounded and a loud buzzing noise came from the dildo. That thing was like a sex machine intent on bringing destruction. How in the world was she supposed to take something like that on?

The sound of Aleck chuckling had her lifting her gaze and to stare at him. His smile was wide as he turned the dildo off and set it beside her. Nothing was said for several long moments, and then he moved between her thighs. She thought he would eat her out like the other men had, but instead he just stared at her pussy.

"Such a pretty pink cunt you have. I bet you'd like me to lick it, wouldn't you?" He lifted his gaze to hers, demanding an answer.

"Yes."

"Yes what?" Voice gone sterner, Aleck's expression flickered between amusement and dominance.

"Yes, Master Aleck."

"Mmmm, I like how that sounds, but I'm afraid that would just be giving in to your pleasure, sweetling." Attention turned back to her vagina, he placed his hand on her inner thighs, perilously close to what she wanted him to touch most.

The torture of feeling his warm breath slide over her clit drove her mad. She let her head fall back on the bed and made her palms into fists. Lalita could feel his thumbs running slow circles at the junction where her pussy and thighs met, and it was excruciating trying not to beg him to touch more of her. Those deft thumbs started moving in faster circles, and she found it hard to stay still. With every puff of breath against the swollen bud of her clit, she could feel herself falling over the edge into oblivion.

Pussy now sopping wet, she knew he could see the cream of her arousal coat her labia and slide down the crack of her ass. Would asking him for what she wanted end up getting her punished? It was tempting to test it out and see what happened, but before the words left her mouth, she felt him move away.

Opening her eyes was harder than she thought. The drug of desire ran through her veins and made her feel euphoric and lethargic all in the same breath. He held the ball gag in his hand and smiled. "I promise to take things slow."

The bed dipped when he moved closer to her. The ball gag was like a beacon of what was to come. Whether that be good or bad, she wasn't quite sure. When the gag was securely attached around her head, he moved off the bed and grabbed the dildo. A smile tilted half of his sensuous mouth and gave him almost a youthful expression.

"I bet I can guess what you want." The tip of the dildo touched her heated pussy, and she moaned around the rubber ball. "I bet you want me to fuck you, don't you?"

Nodding, because that was all she could do, she wished she could beg him to give it to her good and hard. Where was this wanton attitude coming from? She was acting like a crazed, sex-starved teenager. The restraints, the anal plug, and the gag all did something to her, made her desire something darker, naughtier. It made her want things she had never thought she wanted.

Oh, she knew what he wanted to hear, and she was happy to oblige. Her body was on fire and only he could wash out the flames.

His smile returned tenfold. "I knew once you were under my control you'd bend to my will. What a beautiful prisoner you make, Lalita." He positioned himself between her thighs once again and ran the tip of the dildo over her clit. The shock wave that went through her at the small act was instantaneous.

"Close your eyes and let me show you how good it can be."

When her eyes were shut, she felt the smooth, round head of the dildo press against her pussy. He slid it into her with ease at first, and when she arched her back and tried to spread her legs wider, he shoved the rest into her hard and fast. The force had her snapping her eyes open and a moan of pure unadulterated lust coursed through her. Never had she felt something so powerful.

The force and determination had her nipples tightening in response and her pussy clenching around the girth of the dildo. In and out he thrust the dildo, faster and faster until she thought she would pass out from the ecstasy. The slippery sound of her cunt sucking at it was enough to bring her off, but Aleck's deep words demanding that she refrain had her holding off with every ounce of strength she possessed.

As he pumped her pussy full of rubber, she felt the hard slap of his hand across her breasts. The tissue jiggled from the force, and she thrust her breast out for more. The pain accompanied with the pleasure was a screaming duo that had her pumping her hips in time with his thrusting. The restraints did well to keep her legs wide open, but there was enough slack that she could bend her knees and beg, without words, for more. She wondered if he had planned that.

Over and over he slapped her tits, alternating from one to the other until she knew they had to be as red as ripened cherry tomatoes. She wanted to see, wanted to see the outcome of his passion painted across her skin. When she looked down, she could see angry red handprints scattered over her pale flesh. The sight alone was an erotic aphrodisiac that had her wanting it to end but also had her wanting more of his lovely torture.

When he turned the dildo on, it wasn't the buzzing noise of the vibrator that had her body going rigid. She could actually feel the head rotate inside of her. The beads pressed against her inner walls and had lust lighting up every one of her cells. The sensation was incredible, alluring, and tantalizing all in the same moment. She pleaded for more, but all that accomplished was the dildo getting pulled out of her. Aleck left her lying there to feel the aftermath of his sensual abuse.

When she was finally able to open her eyes, she watched him toss the dildo onto the bed. He reached over and grabbed the whip that was nothing more than a handle and several leather straps.

"This is a cat-o'-nine. It isn't the biggest one I have, but for what I have in mind right now, it will work."

There was no time for her to contemplate what he was going to do with it because in the next second he brought those leather straps down across her abdomen. The sting made her eyes water, but when those straps moved against her pussy and breasts in a darkly pleasure-filled motion, she wished she had the gag out to scream for more.

Oh, she wanted a lot more, and a lot harder. The sting of that leather coming into contact with her flesh never receded, but instead morphed into ecstasy. Tears streamed down the side of her face, but it wasn't from fear or pain. It was from wonder and adoration. Was this what she had been missing all her life? Was this the key that would open her eyes and show her that sex was so different than anything she had ever had? Whatever it was, she didn't want it to end.

When he stopped whipping her, she peeled her eyes open and looked down her body. Angry red welts crisscrossed over her pale flesh, adding a splash of his dominance to her body so that although they would heal, she would never forget. She lifted her gaze to him, saw him undoing his pants, and felt her pulse quicken.

The sight of his big fingers slowly undoing the button and sliding the zipper down had her mouth going so dry it was like she swallowed sand. When his pants were down enough he could pull his cock out, she thought her heart stopped. He had fucked her ass, true, but she had yet to actually see the monster flesh that had plowed in and out of her body. His cock was so long and thick it rivaled the other men tenfold. *Damn, and I thought the others were big.*

Pants hanging low on his hips, he gripped his shaft and stroked it as he watched her. He grabbed the bottle of lube with his free hand, uncapped it, and let the cool slickness of it drip on her overheated pussy. She thought she was wet enough, but after getting a look at the anaconda he had been hiding, she knew she would need more than just her own wetness to make his way easy.

Situated between her thighs, Aleck ran his hands up and down her thighs. He would get oh-so-close to her cunt, but just when she thought he would touch it, he would slide those nimble fingers back down her thighs. It was a tease that had her wanting to pull him to her and beg him to fuck her good and hard.

His thighs pressed against hers, the leather sliding against the slickness of her sweaty legs. He started stroking himself again, prolonging what she hoped was the inevitable.

Lalita pulled on her restraints, not knowing if she was trying to get away or move closer to him. Hard pants of breath fell from his lips as he systematically touched her cunt and moved his other palm over his cock. Beads of sweat formed on his brow and chest. The light bounced off of them like tiny shards of glass under the sun.

He started rubbing hard and fast circles around her clit. Oh, the pleasure was transforming into something more powerful. She could feel her orgasm starting to rise to the surface and knew she wouldn't be able to stop it. And right when she thought she couldn't take any more, he stopped touching her and thrust his cock inside of her so hard and fast she saw stars.

The scream that had been building inside of her since the moment he started broke free, but the gag muffled the sound. Straining on her restraints, she tossed her head back as far as it would go and let her orgasm wash through her. His cock tunneled in and out of her, yet she was so gone with her climax that she couldn't even register the sheer size of him stretching and filling her.

The sound of him roaring out his own release vaguely penetrated her mind before blackness washed through her and sent her away into oblivion.

Chapter Nine

What woke Lalita was the sound of something whirling right beside her head. The sensation of floating penetrated her mind, and she pried her eyes open. Everything that had transpired right before she blacked out rushed forward. She blinked several times to try and clear her vision, but it was no use because she couldn't see through the darkened room anyway.

There were no spotlights highlighting the bed or the sex-toy table, and the only light that penetrated the inky darkness was a dimly lit one right above her head which also worked to alter her vision.

When she got her bearings, she realized she was in some kind of chair-like device. She hadn't noticed it earlier, but then again she had been too stunned by all the sexual paraphernalia to notice everything.

Her hands were secured with something behind her back. Both of her legs were bent on each side of her and tied down. Around her breasts was some kind of bra, but it did nothing for support and showed everything she had. Holes were cut out of the leather cups, and her areola and nipples protruded out of the too-small slots. The tissue that showed looked swollen and red, as if the space wasn't big enough and the blood was being cut off.

Upon further investigation, she noticed an elastic band around each of her thighs and one around her abdomen. Several clips hung from strings attached to the bands on her thighs, and a scary one with teeth hung from the band around her middle. A small table beside her held a paddle that looked just big enough to fit in her hand and a bowl covered with a cloth. Aleck was nowhere to be found, but she could sense him watching her. She tried the restraints that secured her hands, and although there was leeway, it was a secure fit.

"I meant to let you rest longer, but I grew too excited to see you in the chair." Aleck stepped out of the darkness. He was completely nude, his cock so hard it was like he hadn't already gotten off.

He stopped right in front of her and ran his finger down the bridge of her nose. Nothing else was said, but there were no words needed when he started to attach the clips to her. She watched with her anxiety growing when he spread one side of her pussy until her labia was pulled completely to the side. He then attached one of the clips to the tender skin. There was a slight pinch of discomfort, but once he attached another one on the same side and then repeated the process on her other labia, warmth bloomed within her.

Next he took the sharp-looking clip that was attached to the band around her waist and secured it on her clit. The initial shock of the teeth on the clip pinching the tender bud had her gasping, but an angry look from Aleck had her biting her tongue and all other noises from her ceasing.

Her vantage point gave her a prime look at what her pussy looked like with all the gadgets attached to her. Both her labia were spread wide so that the inner red of her lips was out in stark relief. The clip on her clit had the bundle of nerves pinched tight so that blood flow was restricted. Lalita swore she could feel her heart beating in her clit, pulsing in time with the blood coursing through her body. As if all of that stuff wasn't enough, Aleck took two other clips she hadn't noticed that were attached to the one on her clit and tethered it up and attached them to her nipples.

When he was all done, he took a step back and smiled widely. She could only imagine the sight he was looking at. She shifted her upper body slightly and felt her eyes widen as the movement caused the straps attached to her nipples to tug on the one attached to her clit. A zing of pleasure and pain slammed into her, and she clenched her fists tightly to stem off the groan that would have fallen from her lips.

A glance back at Aleck confirmed that his sight was trained on her cunt. He stroked himself lazily for a moment before moving between her splayed thighs once again. Although Lalita had come so hard already, she felt herself grow moist for him. Her body had a mind of its own, one where it was crazed for cock, and nothing else would suffice.

She thought he would fuck her by the position he was in, but instead he reached behind her back and undid her hands. Confusion bloomed within her, but he didn't leave her wondering long what his intentions were. Once she had her hands in front of her he took a step back.

"Tying your hands wasn't a necessity, but it was a visual enticement to see you all strung up like my sex slave." He stroked his cock several times before continuing. "Spank my pretty pussy."

What? The ball gag was no longer in her mouth, but she still couldn't talk, not after what he just said.

"Do. As. I. Said." Voice gone harder and sterner, Lalita lifted her hand and brought it down on her exposed vagina. It wasn't a hard slap, but that was a sensitive area down there, and the action made her eyes water.

"Do it harder." Cock in his hand, Aleck pumped his cock faster as he watched what she did between her thighs.

She closed her eyes and did as he said. Whenever her hand landed on her pussy, the clamps would dig into her skin, biting, stinging, arousing. Her open hand on her cunt hurt at first, and although the pain didn't lessen with each sharp whack, she could feel the tissue growing more sensitive and tender. She felt her desire grow.

He let her do this for several more seconds and then ordered her to stop. He walked to the table, picked up the small studded paddle, and handed to her. He then unclamped the clip from her clit but left the others in place. Nothing was said for several prolonged moments.

She looked at that paddle he held in front of her face.

"Ask me."

Ask him? Oh, how he did like his games. What she thought must be clearly written across her face. "What do you plan on using that for?" Oh, she had a pretty good idea what he wanted to use that for. Even now, her cunt throbbed with remembrance of the abuse she just delivered.

He held the paddle out to her, and when she did nothing but stare at it, he raised a brow in question. The handle was made of leather, and when she gripped it, the material was already warmed from his touch.

"Spank your pussy with it."

She snapped her eyes to his and nearly dropped the paddle. "What?"

"You heard me." His tone held no room for argument, and when he crossed his arms over his chest and just stared at her, she knew he was serious.

"Wh–where?" His chuckle did not enlighten or ease her. Oh, she knew where he wanted her to spank, but the very idea of bringing the studded board across her already sore and swollen vagina was a little frightening.

"Don't ask me silly questions, sweetling. Do it now, or I promise you if I do it, you will regret it."

She knew he would make it pleasurable, but she also knew there would be more pain than she would give herself if he had the paddle. Finding the courage to perform the act was easier to think than to actually do, but she didn't want to waste any more time and risk bringing his wrath down upon her.

Paddle gripped tightly in her hand, she lifted it over her pussy.

"And, Lalita?" His voice had dropped to a deep whisper. "If you don't do it hard enough, I'll give you ten extra lashes with my bare hand." The flash of his straight white teeth in the darkness had her swallowing with a touch of fear and excitement.

Her hand had been bad enough, but this was going to be torture. Without thinking about it anymore and talking herself out of it, she brought the paddle down on her pussy. A flash of pain had her arching her back. Electricity slammed into her as the nipple clamps pulled slightly and the hard little buds pulsed.

"Ask me for more."

Already her breathing was increased and her vision blurry. "More, Master Aleck. Please let me have more." Eyes watering, she brought the paddle down on her pussy again when he nodded.

Over and over she did this, crying out in pain and pleasure, begging to be fucked, begging to come, but not finding any release. Her own pussy cream was starting to make the paddle slip across her abused pussy. It was impossible for her to find the orgasm she so desperately wanted. Cunt tender and tingling from the abuse, her whole body shook. It took all her strength to hold onto the handle and continue to spank herself.

As if he had read her mind, he took the paddle from her and undid the clips on her labia and nipples. Eyes closed and head resting on the back of the chair, Lalita panted in exertion. When she felt Aleck's hot, wet mouth on her sensitive cunt, she sighed in bliss. The wetness and heat soothed her aching flesh. He latched onto her clit and sucked feverishly until she inadvertently gripped his hair between her fingers and ground her pussy into his face, well, as much as she could given the position she was in.

She could hear movement beside her but didn't have the strength to open her eyes and investigate. It wasn't until she felt something icy cold replace the warm depth of Aleck's mouth that she gasped. Knowing her eyes were wide, Lalita stared down as Aleck pressed an ice cube to her clit. That small cube melted almost immediately and he grabbed another and ran it over her pussy hole. As if that wasn't enough, he pushed the melting square inside of her, and she moaned at the dual sensations that rocked her.

Hot and cold clashed inside of her, and then water and her cream melted out of her pussy. Aleck was there to lap it up and to repeat the process with the cubes on her clit and nipples.

She couldn't stop thrashing her head from side-to-side, wanting him to stop, wanting him to keep going. Her mind and body were at war over what the other wanted. When he placed another cube on her clit, he immediately latched his mouth over it and sucked. The combination was her undoing, and she came, permission or not. Animal like sounds came from him as he lapped up her orgasm. She was too weak and exhausted to do anything else but lay there, but when she felt him unhooking her feet, she cracked her eyes open. A strange look covered his face, one she didn't want to address at this very moment.

He wrapped his arms around her and held her for several long minutes before moving over to the bed and gently setting her on it. The chill in the air seemed almost frigid to her, and she began to shake. Aleck was right there, holding her, whispering sweet words into her ear, touching her gently.

"My sweet Lalita. How you please me so." He brought his lips to hers for a gentle kiss and held her tightly.

She couldn't help but fall into his embrace. She wanted to be close at this moment, wanted to feel his body heat soaking into her flesh.

"Please, Aleck."

"Shhh. You've been so good. Let me take care of you."

Eyes closed because she just didn't have the strength to keep them open, Lalita felt him smooth his hands over her skin and pull her closer. She spread her thighs to accept his larger frame between them and arched into him. The orgasm she had just moments ago didn't seem to satisfy her, and all she wanted was the closeness of another human body beside her, on her, and in her. She wanted to feel Aleck moving that big cock in her pussy as she clung to him and cried out in ecstasy.

The tip of his shaft nudged her opening. "Look at me, Lalita."

She opened her eyes and stared into the deep depths of his green ones. They were like cut emeralds under the dim light. His blond hair hung in damp strands across his forehead as he stared down at her.

His muscular arms were braced on either side of her head as he pushed into her. It was an incredible feeling to have him penetrate her because it was so different from the other two times he had been intimate with her. This time it actually felt like there was something more between them.

"Touch me." His whispered words teased the shell of her ear.

Finally she would get to feel him under her fingertips. When her arms were braced on his shoulders, he rested more of his upper body on hers. Both of them were slick with perspiration and moved sensually together as he grinded his pelvis against hers. The act wasn't rushed, and as their bodies moved as one and they both came at the same time, it was a feeling of belonging that moved through her. Lalita didn't want to look too deeply into it, but it was an emotion that was too strong to ignore.

He didn't fuck her, he made love to her, and she couldn't have found a better way to end an evening filled with so many dark pleasures.

Chapter Ten

Having sex on a continual basis seemed to make the days fly by. She missed Lennon, but thankfully she was allowed to call him on her days off. At least she was comforted by the knowledge that he was happy with Mary and her daughter who was about his age, but still, she missed him something fierce. There was a light at the end of the tunnel, but Lalita was finding it harder and harder not to let her emotions get involved.

Some of the men tended to keep their distance with her unless they wanted some kind of sexual favor. It seemed that only Aleck, Torryn, Michael, and Dorian were the ones that wanted to actually talk to her about other things besides sex.

Torryn was very good at fucking her until she couldn't stand straight and then leaving her to clean up after him, but there were times when he would talk to her as if she hadn't been hired to have sex with them. He talked to her at times like he cared for her as more than just a sexual thing to use to get off with.

Kane and Zakary were colder with her than the other four. It was still hard to look at Aleck after the night they had, but she realized that he was only like that in the bedroom. Outside of it he was the kindest and gentlest out of the six, well, aside from Michael who seemed to like to touch her intimately at every opportunity.

Then there was Dorian, the strong silent type that, although he spoke to her and asked her about *her*, still kept his distance and his emotions hidden. Sex with him was always dominating and memorable and, she admitted to herself, sometimes almost seemed possessive. With each passing day, she realized her emotions had a mind of their own, but she was good to keep them to herself and not let them show.

The day was beautiful, and she planned on spending her "free" time exploring the grounds and maybe even trying out the impressive hedge maze. No one was in sight when she made her way downstairs and out the backdoor. Although they had specifically said she couldn't bring anything with her, the small suitcase she had brought held a few items of clothing and personal mementos, like a picture of her son. Thankfully the things she brought hadn't been taken from her.

Dressed in a pair of jeans and a cardigan set, she actually felt like a woman. On her other days off, she had been so thoroughly exhausted that she hadn't even contemplated going outside and seeing the grounds, but today she forced herself to get dressed and get some fresh air.

As soon as she opened the back door she closed her eyes and let the warm rays of the sun absorb into her skin. A light breeze whistled by and shifted her hair that hung across her shoulders. She closed the door behind her and took a step off the landing. The estate was monstrous, and the surrounding land wasn't any different. Directly in front of her sat the table where she and Aleck had shared dinner. Beyond that was the hedge maze. To the left was an opulent swimming pool, and to the right was a vast garden that was intricately landscaped. There had to be hundreds upon hundreds of varying flowers in that garden. Although it was tempting to head toward the flowers, Lalita really wanted to try out the maze.

The front entrance showed a sign inlaid in black stone of an aerial view of the maze. It wasn't overly large, but there were enough twists and turns that someone could easily get lost in there for hours. The thought that maybe this wasn't a good idea played in her head, but curiosity won over and Lalita headed forward.

It was clear the maze, as well as the grounds, was kept up with precision and detail. Not a single twig or leaf was out of place as she made her way through the winding maze. Who actually took care of the grounds was a mystery to her since she never saw any staff, but it was clear someone was taking care of things. She couldn't help but think that Lennon would love this place with all the nooks and crannies the mansion had to offer and all the things he could explore outside. She hated thinking about her son while at the estate because all it did was make her depressed and guilty. Over and over she wondered if she was a bad mother for leaving him to go fuck a bunch of men. Sure, her intentions might have been good, but it still didn't make her feel any better.

Would she ever be able to look him in the eye after what she did? It was true she would have enough money to keep him happy and comfortable, but she knew where that money would have come from. Shaking the thoughts from her mind, she pressed forward.

A stone bench greeted her when she turned a corner, as well as a dead end. When she sat down, the coldness of the stone was startling, but it wasn't enough to distract her from her thoughts.

Tears started to fall down her cheeks as she thought about her predicament. "It doesn't do any good wallowing in your own self-pity when you put yourself in this position." She wiped her tears away and sat up straighter. "Act like a woman and do your job. You can worry about how you'll feel later. Right now you know what your objective is. Man up, Lalita."

Talking to herself didn't help, but the silliness of what she was doing put a smile on her face.

There really was no reason to cry over the choices she made. And in all honesty, she couldn't feel that sorry for herself. She had met some amazing men and, despite her better judgment, was starting to feel things that maybe she shouldn't.

Lalita stood up and started through the maze again. The tranquility and serenity of her surroundings had her mind wandering to different things, things that didn't make her cry.

* * * *

Hours passed, and Lalita still couldn't find her way out of the maze. *Great fucking idea.* The frustration just kept building and building until she thought she would scream. She tried to visualize the map at the front entrance, but her head hurt and she couldn't think clearly. The crying had started an hour ago and hadn't relented. Overall this had been a horrible idea.

She had tried to see over the wall by standing on a bench, but it was no use. The hedges were too high and she was just too short. Climbing the wall wasn't even an option because, well, there was no leverage. Either find a way out or hope someone came looking for her. As the sun started to descend and everything became dark, visibility was becoming very limited. The only good thing about it getting dark was that she could see the light from the mansion, but even that didn't help her get back. There were just too many twists and turns in the maze that she was thoroughly turned around.

Ass on yet another bench, she rested her head in her hands. Her eyes felt swollen from crying, and her nose was stuffed up so bad she could hardly breathe. Just as she thought she would have to spend the night in the creepy maze, she thought she heard her name being called. Holding her breath in hopes it wasn't just her imagination, she heard it again, closer.

Cupping her hands around her mouth, she shouted as loud as she could. "Over here." Heart beating in excitement, she could hear the sound of heavy footfalls coming closer and closer.

A dark figure stepped around the corner just as a bright beam of light blinded her. She lifted her hand and covered her eyes, wondering which man had found her. When she lowered her hand, she could see that it was Dorian. Although it was dark outside, he was close enough that she could see the strange expression on his face.

"You were lost." Out of breath as if he had been running, he pulled her from the bench and wrapped her in a tight embrace.

Lalita was caught so off guard that she fell back into the hedge. He righted them and stepped away from her.

"We thought you left initially until we saw your suitcase still here." He cleared his throat. "What happened? Why did you come in here without someone else?" No longer did he sound relieved to see her. Anger was starting to replace that emotion.

What could she say? Why did she have to say anything? "It was my free day, and this is what I chose to do. None of you take me out of the house long enough to explore the grounds 'with someone else,' so how am I supposed to know certain things?"

Now her voice was rising because, frankly, who the hell did he think he was, questioning her? Of course she was happy to see him, but he sounded almost accusatory, like she had meant to get herself lost.

He let out a long breath and ran his hand over his jaw. "You're right, and I'm sorry for snapping at you. You just had me worried, had *all* of us worried." He said the last part almost as a filler, as if he hadn't meant to say *he* had worried about her.

"Come on, the others will be happy to know you haven't run off, or worse, fallen over the cliff."

"There's a cliff?" He didn't answer her high-pitched question.

He took hold of her hand and led her back out the way he came. Lalita was embarrassed to realize she had been so close to the entrance that if she hadn't sat down, she probably would have found it. When they exited the maze, she noticed Dorian kept hold of her hand. He placed the flashlight under his arm and pulled out a cell phone.

"Yeah, I found her. She was in the maze." There was a moment of silence, and then Dorian mumbled a few more words before putting his phone back in his pocket.

He pushed the back door open and gently led her inside. A few moments later the front door opened and she heard the other guys call out to them. When they were all in the entertainment room, the other five stared at her, some angrily, some with relieved expressions on their faces.

Lalita said the only thing that came to mind. "Sorry." A terse moment passed, and then Aleck chuckled. Torryn and Michael looked more at ease, but she could see an underlying emotion of anger cross Torryn's face. Zakary and Kane remained angry looking and refused to meet her gaze.

"Well, I'm starving, so let's eat." Aleck rubbed his hands together and went into the kitchen, but not before stopping beside her and kissing her on the cheek. "I'm glad you didn't fall over the cliff." He leaned back, winked, and followed a tense Zakary and Kane out.

When it was just Dorian and her, she turned and looked up at him. "I'm really sorry I ruined your night and made everyone mad. That wasn't my intention. I just wanted to see the maze." She was sorry in a way because now it was going to be awkward as hell around them.

Dorian didn't speak right away, and when he did, she was surprised by his response. "I know, love. Don't mind Zakary, Torryn, and Kane."

Michael started to chuckle and then leaned in and kissed her on the forehead. "They are always pissed about something." Michael followed the other men and left her and Dorian alone.

Dorian leaned in and brought his lips to hers. The kiss lasted several seconds, and Lalita could feel her toes curl with pleasure. He broke the kiss all too soon and headed into the kitchen. Although she liked her nights off, she wouldn't mind finishing what Dorian had started. It was a nice thought, one that she might have to act on. A smile curled her lips. She may have signed up to be their submissive, but she didn't see anything in the contract that said she couldn't seduce them herself in her free time.

Chapter Eleven

It was not surprising that every time she had a night off the men went to bed early. She retired early herself, but not so she could rest up. Ever since the idea to seduce Dorian played in her mind, she hadn't been able to get rid of it. She had been given equal time with each man, but there was something about Dorian that made her want to see more of him.

It was a crazy notion, but the very image of slipping into his room while he slept, sliding beneath the covers beside him, and running her hands over all that muscle was too tempting to resist. If she was smart, she would have soaked in the tub longer to ease her muscles, but the excitement of what she was going to do tonight had her quickly washing and primping.

Even though she had been intimate with Dorian on several occasions, never once did she explore his body as he did hers. Tonight may be no different, but it wouldn't hurt to try. Could he really punish her if she was doing this on a night that was dubbed "her free night"? Time would tell.

Dressed in only a long ivory silk chemise, Lalita slipped out of her room and made her way toward the room that Dorian stayed in. The walls and doors were thick, and she doubted anyone could hear her creeping around in the hallway, but she made sure not make any unnecessary noise.

When she was in front of the twin oak doors of Dorian's room, she froze. Nerves frazzled because of her intent, she didn't know what to do. A glance down each side of the hallway assured her that she was alone, and the ominous sound of the grandfather clock downstairs ticking away was in tune with the pulse beating in her neck. *It's now or never.*

The doorknob was freezing when she gripped it. Turning it as silently as she could, Lalita pushed the door open just enough to squeeze through. The room was pitch black once she closed the door behind her. Back pressed against the unyielding wood, she tried to calm her rapid breathing. Once her eyesight adjusted, she was able to make out the bed and the large form beneath the covers.

Tiptoeing across the plushly carpeted floor, she stopped once she reached the side of the bed that was vacant. *Oh God. You can do this. Stop being a coward.* The only movement from Dorian was the steady rise and fall of his chest. Teeth clenched as she crawled into bed, she was at least thankful it was king-sized and her movement barely rattled the other side.

Once she was under the covers, she didn't know what do to next. She was close enough to him that she could smell the aftershave he wore and see the smooth curve of his shoulder. Not wasting another minute, she lifted her hand to run her fingers along the hard contours of his arm. Before she made contact, she was thrown on her back and a hard body was pressed on top of her.

Dorian stared down at her with a mixture of confusion and curiosity. "What are you doing here, Lalita?"

She licked her lips and noticed how his gaze dropped down to watch the movement. Should she tell him the truth? Should she tell him what her intentions had been?

"I came to seduce you." Voice no more than a whisper, she knew how she must have looked to him. Her eyes must have been huge, her breathing erratic, and body tense.

He felt so heavy atop her, his big arms and legs pinning her to the mattress, so escape was impossible. If she was being honest, she would have to admit that she had no intentions of escaping.

"You snuck in my room in the middle of the night to seduce me?" One dark brow rose and a smirk curled his lips. "Interesting." He dipped his head and ran his lips over her throat.

She heard him inhale deeply and wondered if he could smell the lavender perfume she had used just for this occasion. He shifted on top of her so that she was forced to spread her legs wider to accommodate him. When she felt the hard length of his erection press against her silk-clad pussy, she nearly groaned. Despite the thin barrier of their clothing, it was too much of a distraction. Lalita wanted to feel his skin sliding against hers, but he had the upper hand at the moment. Seemed her seducing skills had gone to shit.

First he slipped one of her straps down her arm and then the other. When the silk fell away from her breasts, she heard him inhale deeply, as if he was shocked by the sight. They certainly weren't anything he had never seen before, but she could see him staring down at them as if it was the first time he had looked at her nude.

Taking control had been her motive in coming here, but it seemed Dorian was taking matters into his own hands. He cupped one of her breasts and dipped his head to take her nipple into his mouth. His movements were unhurried, and she absorbed the feeling of just being touched by a man she had grown to care for. It still seemed strange that she could feel this strongly about him in such a short period of time.

He alternated between breasts until she could hear herself panting and thrusting the twin mounds more firmly into his face. The rest of her gown was next to come off, and then he removed his boxers. A deep sigh left her when she finally felt his nude body flush with hers. There were no hurried movements as he touched and kissed every part of her body.

When he rolled onto his back and pulled her atop him, she felt like a queen as he stared up at her.

"Take control, seductress." A wicked grin curled his lips.

She reached between their bodies and grabbed his cock. It felt so hot in her hand, like velvet-coated, warmed steel. Lifting onto her knees, she positioned the tip of his erection at the entrance of her pussy and slowly sank down. The deep breath he exhaled once he was fully inside of her was one of content. Maybe she was reading too much into it, and maybe he was just fucking her like every other time, but it sure didn't feel that way.

Hands braced on his pectoral muscles, Lalita lifted off so that his cockhead almost slipped out, and then she pushed back down. Legs on each side of his muscular thighs and the power to control the pace, Lalita felt alive. His hands wrapped nearly around her waist, and he lifted up enough to run his tongue along the underside of her throat and up to her ear.

He whispered against her hair, "Ride me hard, baby."

She rode him like her life depended on it. Up and down, a swivel of her hips, a grind of her pelvis, and she was close to coming. Slick, wet skin slapped together, an almost dirty noise that made her hotter. The combination of their panting and groaning is what finally set her off. Back arched and head thrown back, Lalita cried out as bliss washed through her. Dorian tightened his hands on her waist and thrust into her with all the power he had before stilling and groaning out his own orgasm.

It was the first time since being at the estate that she really regretted what she had just done.

* * * *

Lalita lay beside Dorian with her head on his chest. The sound of his heart beating was enough to lull her to sleep, but she didn't want to miss any of her time with him. This one moment she didn't feel like a sex object. She felt like a woman that had just made love with a man, and there was that comfortable silence between them.

Because of her feelings for Dorian and how they seemed to be escalating, she did have a twinge of regret over her decision. For one thing, she seemed to be more attached to Dorian than the other men. Dorian wasn't the only one she was really starting to have feelings for, though. Aleck and Torryn were slowly wedging their way inside of her heart. Even though there were times were Torryn seemed distant with her, as if the only thing between them was sex, there were also times he seemed like he truly cared.

Despite telling herself over and over again that she shouldn't feel anything, she couldn't help herself. The time she had just spent with Dorian didn't help.

Dorian ran the tips of his fingers up and down her back and brought her back from her thoughts. It soothed and calmed her, and she wished this moment would never end. It was agony and ecstasy to lie beside a man she had just been intimate with. It was agony because she knew there was no way he could harbor the same feelings she had for him. What man could care about a woman that he paid to have sex with him and five other men?

"Can I ask you a question?" She worried about how he would answer.

"Sure."

"Why did you choose me out of all the other applicants?" Hell. She put it like she had applied for a regular job. The silence that greeted her was not comforting, but he didn't stop running his fingers over her back, so she took it as a good sign.

"To be honest? I don't know."

Nice. Instantly she felt mortified for even asking. She went to move away because the closeness was just too much now, but he placed his hand flat on her back and stopped any and all movements.

"You misunderstand." It always amazed her that he seemed to know exactly what she thought. He turned to look at her but kept his hand on her back. "There were many beautiful women that had done this previously who applied, but there was something about you."

They had since turned on the small bedside lamp, and the shadows played across his face.

"We were all speechless when you walked in wearing that little dress. You didn't even need to get naked for me to know that I wanted you."

Lalita felt her heart skip a beat at his words. He cupped her cheek and leaned in to kiss her softly. Oh, how she wanted to feel like this forever, but she knew as soon as the sun came up she would be fair game for everyone again.

"You getting naked was just me being selfish." She could feel his grin against her mouth. "We tried this situation out before, but my cousins and brother thought the women were too experienced for what they wanted."

Cousins? Brother? Shocked wasn't even the right word for how his words made her feel. Why he even told her this was beyond her, but she was glad for any little piece of information that gave her insight into their lives.

"Wow. Keeping it in the family has a whole new meaning now."

He chuckled deeply. "I can see how that information might be shocking, but you had to have known we were related when you saw the family portrait?"

Thinking back to the day she cut her foot, she remembered the portrait he spoke of. Since then she had kind of put it in the back of her mind, but she supposed she shouldn't feel too shocked now. They did resemble each other one way or another.

"Anyway, I don't know exactly what it was about you that had us all smitten, but we knew you were the one we wanted right from the beginning." He pulled her close so she rested her cheek against his chest once more. He shifted and then the room was doused in darkness. It didn't take very long for Lalita to fall asleep to the sound of the steady beat of Dorian's heart.

Chapter Twelve

"Get on your knees and suck my cock." Torryn stared at her with unflinching hazel eyes. Michael, Kane, and Zakary stayed off to the side, the three of them sated from the blow jobs she had given them.

Lalita was nude, aside from a set of nipple clips that were tethered to a thin chain attached to her clit. Her jaw ached from sucking Michael, Kane, and Zakary's cocks just moments before, but Torryn made no joke about what he wanted. He was especially fierce today, and she couldn't understand why. From his voice to his very demeanor, he screamed uncaring asshole. In the end, she sucked it up and performed. What else was she supposed to do, cry because it was one of those times when he didn't act like he cared for her?

She gripped the root of his shaft and licked the head. He apparently didn't like the tease because he thrust into her mouth with a little more force than was necessary. The tip of his cock hit the back of her throat, and she gagged. He fucked her face then, obviously getting turned on by the sound and very idea of her gagging. Eyes watering, Lalita held on to his thighs and tasted the first hot jets of his cum shooting down her throat.

"Go easy, dude." Kane spoke, but Torryn kept pumping into her.

"Gentle, Tor." Michael was the next to speak, and although his words didn't seem harsh in context, his voice was angry and deep.

"Easy." Zakary mimicked the other two's concern, and finally Torryn pulled his softening dick from her mouth.

He took a step back, and his cum dripped down her chin. She wiped the tears from her eyes but kept her composure. Why did she have to feel this way? She shouldn't have let her emotions get the better of her. A month and a half had already passed, and instead of doing the job she had been hired for, she was feeling emotions she shouldn't. She didn't want to feel like the woman they hired to have sex with them. She wanted to feel like *their* woman.

Lalita wasn't stupid. There was a small sliver of hope inside of her that thought maybe, just maybe, they would feel something for her as well. They were ideal wishes from a demented woman.

Torryn stared down at her for several long seconds. "Kane, Michael, and Zak, give us a moment."

Oh hell. He was already in a foul mood, and she didn't know how she felt about it just being the two of them. The three of them hesitated but finally left. She had no idea what Torryn's problem was, but it was clear something bothered him. When he sat on the couch and breathed out deeply, the empathy in her screamed out to comfort him. He looked like a failed man. His head hung, and his back was curled forward.

"Lalita, come here." He didn't look at her when he spoke.

The words were so low Lalita thought she had heard wrong at first. When he finally lifted his gaze to hers, she was struck by emotions. It was clear he was reining in his feelings, but he couldn't hide the anguish behind his eyes.

"Come here. Please." He patted the seat next to him, and she got up to move toward him.

Bones aching from being on her knees, she was mindful of the clit and nipple clips as she sat next to him. The silence between them was so thick she could have cut it with a knife. After what seemed like forever, he turned to face her and took the clamps off her body. Blood rushed back to the tender areas. He handed her a blanket, and she gratefully wrapped it around her body.

"I have to apologize for the way I've treated you." He stared at her as if he expected her to say something, but she was speechless.

What could she say? *True, you have been an ass to me, but I can't fault you when you have no right to feel anything for me.* Yeah, she could see that going over real well. Instead, she kept her mouth shut and looked down like the good submissive. Torryn's finger under her chin had her lifting her head and staring into his tormented eyes.

"I know saying sorry doesn't make up for how I've acted, but I suppose it's a start." He smiled almost hesitantly. "You see, I just went through a really nasty divorce. It isn't about the money she swindled out of me, but a fact I learned far too late. My personal problems don't excuse me for the way I've acted, but I want to explain *why* I've acted this way."

Whatever he was talking about caused his voice to grow husky. Not thinking and just acting on wanting to make him feel better, Lalita placed her hand on top of his. He looked up at her as if startled, but then smiled.

"I'm listening." She wanted him to know that whatever he was going through, he could unleash. She knew all about heartache and sorrow, and she wouldn't have been able to get through it if not for people who cared about her and showed her support.

"I don't open up to people about my problems, but there is something about you that draws me. I feel the need to lay it all out for you."

"Sometimes you need an unbiased ear to vent to, and sometimes you need comfort." She hoped he got her hint.

He was silent for a suspended moment and then finally spoke. "After the divorce, because my ex is a spiteful and hateful bitch, she informed me that she was pregnant by another man. Turned out that the 'other man' was my partner and best friend." He cleared his throat and shifted on the couch.

Lalita knew that what he was about to say next was what had been causing him so much grief.

"She left out that little detail until the divorce was finalized. In this state, if a woman is pregnant, a judge won't grant the divorce, on the grounds that the husband is presumed the father." Torryn's head was lowered, but Lalita still saw the lone tear slide down his cheek.

"I suppose I could have fought it, but I just wanted to be done with her. She knew how much I wanted children, but over and over again she said she didn't want them. I thought I could live with that, had even convinced myself." Torryn wiped his face and cleared his throat as if he didn't want her to know how much he hurt.

"My hatred for her has cost me a lot. I have grown angry and resentful, and I think inadvertently I have carried that over to you and everyone around me." He placed his hand on her cheek. "These guys put up with me because I'm family, but if that wasn't the case, I know they would have kicked my ass out the door long ago. I can only say that I am sincerely sorry for making you feel less than what you are. Do you accept my apology?"

Lalita hadn't even known she was crying until she felt Torryn wipe the tears away from her cheek. His admission was heartfelt and honest. How could she stay angry when he poured his heart out to her?

"I'm not angry with you, and I accept your apology." He wrapped her in a tight embrace, and she finally felt warmth from him.

When he started kissing her neck and then moved to her mouth, a different kind of warmth bloomed within her. He shifted on the couch and she felt his cock stiffen against her thigh. Her pussy became moist as her still-sensitive nipple rubbed against his smooth, muscular chest. This didn't feel like sex, no, it felt like making love. It was soft, gentle, and easy. His hands were everywhere, stroking, caressing, drawing her deeper and deeper into an intense arousal she almost couldn't bear it.

He pressed his bigger body against hers until she was lying on the couch. Her legs were spread and she wrapped them around his waist. She was wet enough he could have shoved all those thick inches into her and it would have been as smooth as butter.

He murmured against her lips, "I want this to last, Lalita." He ran his tongue along the seam of her lips. "Put me inside of you, baby."

Doing what he asked without any hesitation, Lalita gripped his erection and put it at the entrance of her body. He sank fully into her, and she arched her back and sighed. The only sound either of them made while her pumped his cock into her pussy was heavy panting and blissful sighs. When she climaxed, Torryn did as well.

At that very moment, Lalita felt something inside of him unlock. This moment wasn't about fucking, it was about two people sharing emotions with each other. It was a comforting feeling, but also a frightening one.

* * * *

"I miss you, Momma." Lennon's small voice came through the receiver like a punch to Lalita's gut.

God, how she missed her little man. "Are you having fun with Megan?" Mary's daughter was a year older then Lennon, which made the separation a little easier for him. At least he had someone to play with.

"Yeah, but I miss you. When are you coming home?"

"I miss you, too, baby. I'll be home before you know it." Holding in her tears was harder then she thought. "Be good for Auntie Mary, okay?"

"I am always good, Momma."

"I know, sweetie."

Her time at the estate was drawing to an end, and despite the revelations, feelings, and emotions that had been developed, it was clear everyone just wanted to go back to the way it was, including her. It seemed the closer she got to leaving, the more everyone pulled away. In a way it was a relief because it gave her time to focus on what was really important in her life, and she knew that her life as well as theirs didn't include a relationship.

After they hung up, she tried her hardest to hold off the tears, but it didn't help. It felt good to cry, but at the same time it made her feel worse.

It wasn't until the tears really fell that she sensed someone behind her. She wasn't surprised to see Dorian standing in the doorway, but she was surprised to see a sympathetic look on his face.

"You okay?" He pushed off the frame and sat on the edge of her bed.

"Yeah. I was just thinking." She so didn't want him to watch her cry, but him being here was a good way to keep her inner turmoil in check.

He pushed away from the doorframe and held his hand out for her. "Come on."

"It's my day off." Not that she minded if he wanted a little alone time because, truth be told, she wouldn't mind a little closeness, especially with how she was feeling.

He chuckled, and the sound speared right into her body. "I think you need to get out of this house. Let me take you to lunch."

"Really?" He chuckled again and nodded. She barely had enough time to slip on her shoes before he was leading her out of the house and to his car. It was a fancy European SUV that was dark and shiny.

When they were both buckled in, he started the car and headed down the long winding driveway. She had been too stunned on the trip up here to pay attention to her surroundings, but now they took her breath away. The countryside was picturesque and serene.

When they finally made it into town, the scene looked like something out of an eighteenth-century photo. Cobblestone sidewalks and small country-style shops lined each side of the road. People watering hanging flower baskets and setting up fresh fruit stands outside of their cozy shops greeted her.

"This is amazing." She hadn't thought she spoke out loud until Dorian started to speak.

"It really is. It's like this little town hasn't been touched by modern evolution. It was one of the reasons I bought the estate." When he looked over at her and cast her one of his devilish smiles, her heart skipped a beat.

"About fifty miles away is the next town. That has the bigger supermarkets and strip malls, but usually you can get everything you need right here."

When he parked in front of a small bistro and shut off the car, they sat in silence for a moment. "Thanks for taking me out today."

"You looked like you needed to get away from everything for a little bit."

Lalita watched Dorian slip from the car and walk around to open her door. She couldn't help her feelings. She had thought she had pushed them to the back of her mind, but how wrong she had been. It would have been better if he was a big prick, maybe that way she could have ignored how she felt, but when he did things like this, it made keeping her emotions in check impossible.

The door opened almost silently. They stared at each other before he helped her out of the car. She didn't miss how his hand wrapped around her waist almost possessively, or maybe it was just wishful thinking on her part?

"Ready?"

No, she wasn't, but she could pretend.

Chapter Thirteen

Although they had only meant to go for lunch, by the time they returned to the estate it was already dark. The mansion was lit up like a lighthouse for lost boats, and Lalita had a passing feeling that she would miss the estate when she left. It was a stupid and idle thought that was gone as soon as it had popped into her mind.

When they opened the door and walked through, Michael, Kane, Zakary, Aleck, and Torryn were right in their faces.

"What the fuck?" Kane was the first to speak, but all the others looked just as pissed off as he did. "So now you're sneaking in an extra day?" His voice raised an octave.

Lalita could smell the whiskey that coated his breath. In fact, she could smell alcohol on each of them as they spouted off angry comments about her spending extra time with Dorian.

"Lalita, go upstairs." Dorian didn't look at her when he spoke, but all the other men did.

"Oh hell no. She can stay right here and listen to what we have to say." Zakary stepped beside Kane, his eyes glossy and red-rimmed.

"I said go upstairs, Lalita." Dorian did look at her then, and his expression spoke volumes.

Not waiting another minute, she turned and started for the stairs when a strong arm gripped her wrist and halted her.

"She can stay. If she wants to use her free time to fuck you behind our backs, then she can give each of us a little extra time." Zakary pulled her to him, and the bags she held fell to the ground.

He wasn't rough with her, but his hand on her wrist was unyielding. She did not want to be around a bunch of men that were intoxicated. When she looked over at Dorian, she could see his eyes were on where Zakary held her wrist. His jaw was clenched and his fists were balled.

Michael gripped Zakary's hand, and the two of them stared each other down. "Let her go, Zakary. If you want to handle this like men, then we can," he said through clenched teeth.

"What do you think you're going to do, pin her to the ground and mount her like some whore in a back alley?" Dorian followed up Michael with his own angry response.

Everyone grew silent, and she felt the hold on her wrist loosen.

"Let her go, Zak. Dorian and Michael are right. We're all acting like a bunch of assholes." Aleck spoke up for the first time, and although it was clear he had been drinking, too, he seemed soberest out of the others.

Zak let go of her wrist, and she could see a splash of red cover his face. He was either embarrassed or even more pissed over the situation. She assumed it was the latter.

She knew this wasn't the place for her, but she also knew she didn't want any of them fighting. Anger and concern over the situation were dual emotions that rose with each passing second inside of her.

"Lalita, please go upstairs." There was almost a pleading tone in Dorian's voice.

She picked up her bags and made her way up the stairs, very aware that all their eyes were on her. When she reached the landing, she headed off to her room, but she didn't make it inside. They couldn't see her from the position she was in, and there was no way in hell she could *not* listen to what they were about to say.

"What the hell? Looks like you wanted a little extra time with her." Zakary's voice was clipped, and despite it being pitched low, Lalita could hear his words clearly.

"I didn't realize what she did on her free time was anyone else's concern." Dorian's voice, ever the calm and stern tone, brooked no argument.

"It does matter when you're fucking her behind our backs. We already only get one day a week, and here you are taking an extra day." Slurred, angry words came from Torryn. "We each are entitled to the same amount of time with her."

Lalita edged closer to the banister but made sure to keep out of sight. The scene below looked hot and angry, and she knew if things didn't calm down between the guys, it was going to get a lot worse.

"I have to agree with them, Dorian." Aleck stepped in front of him, his composure easygoing.

"We talked about being fair in this agreement when we first decided to go through with it." Michael interjected. "I don't want her feeling like a piece of meat, but fair is fair, Dor."

Even from her vantage point, Lalita could see Dorian's clenched jaw. "Like I said before, what she does on her personal time is no one else's concern. I didn't see any of you taking the time to show her around. You have been more worried about fucking her until she can't stand straight. I thought she would enjoy a nice day in town, which she did."

Kane pointed a finger at Dorian's chest. "So you mean to tell me she didn't sneak into your room, and you guys didn't screw?"

By the outraged murmurs, it was clear the other guys had no idea about her little nighttime visit with Dorian. Embarrassment coursed through her. She had thought she had been sneaky, but it was clear she hadn't been the only one up that night.

"I'm not going to repeat myself to a drunk." Dorian headed toward the parlor, when Kane's words stopped him in his tracks and had her breath stalling.

"You're letting your feelings for her override your better judgment."

Dorian turned and leveled a dark stare at Kane. "You need to shut the fuck up right now, Kane."

"Why should I? You don't think we haven't noticed the way you look at her? May I remind you she is being *paid* to be here? She is our *employee*. It would do you some good to remember that."

There was a hushed silence that fell over the room. What Kane said was the truth, but she couldn't lie and say it didn't sting hearing it directly from the source. Casting her stare at Dorian, she wanted to know what he was thinking at that moment. He didn't make her wait long.

"All of you can rest assured that there is no emotional attachment with this situation. We hired her to fuck, I understand that, but her being cooped up in here the whole time isn't good for anyone. I took her out today for no other reason than we both had to eat and she needed to get out of the house." His voice hadn't raised an octave, but his stare was dark. "My feelings for her run as deep as whether or not it is my turn to fuck her." With that being said, Dorian turned and stalked into the parlor.

The other five men murmured too softly for her to hear, but it didn't matter. Dorian's words had been like a knife in her gut. Last night and today, it seemed like some of them had mirrored her feelings. It was painfully clear she had been a fool.

Mortification washed through her at how stupid she had been. Men like that didn't fall for woman like her. They wanted unattached supermodels, not single mothers that had to make extra money doing "side jobs." All she wanted to do was crawl under a rock and die of embarrassment.

When she forced herself to go back to her room, she could only sit on her bed and stare at the wall. She was just glad she had less than two weeks left. Any longer and she didn't know if she could bear it. It was already going to be difficult, not to mention horrifying, to see the guys every day. *Nice mess you've gotten yourself into.*

Chapter Fourteen

It was the night before Lalita's last day at the estate, and she was looking forward to going back home. Ever since the drunken situation with Dorian and the other guys, things just hadn't been the same. Despite the fact they were obviously trying to appear like nothing bothered them, it wasn't hard for her to see the way they didn't speak to her as much and the way they did everything in their power to make the rest of her stay as unemotional as possible.

It wasn't like she shouldn't expect this, but with each passing day, and with each intimate encounter with the guys, Lalita was feeling like she had been foolish to think there had been anything more in this agreement than just sex.

Dorian, Michael, Torryn, and Aleck had been especially distant with her, and the fact that those were the four that she had grown the most attached to really hurt. It was Dorian's night, one she had been dreading the entire week. They hadn't had sex since she had "seduced" him and there had been the confrontation with the other men. She tried to act as if she didn't realize the fact they hadn't had sex it and it didn't bother her. Both were an obvious lie.

When she had gotten out of the bathroom that morning, she had discovered a note lying on her bed. It had been from Dorian, with specific instructions. Like always, her pussy was to be completely shaved, and she was to wear the items enclosed in the box on her bed. It wasn't too much of a surprise when she opened the box and found a lacy little bra with the nipples cut out of the fabric, an anal plug, a bottle of lube, and a belt that attached to a set of garters.

Once the bra and garters were on, she looked at herself in the mirror. Her hair was still damp from her bath and started to curl at the ends. The strands teased her bare nipples, which in turn made them protrude even farther out of the bra. The anal plug was the last thing she even touched because frankly it was intimidating as hell. It was just as large as the one Aleck had used on her, but there was something about this particular plug that worried her.

It was long and clear and slightly thicker at the base. It had a series of snaps on the bottom of it which matched the ones on the garters and belt that went across her abdomen. She knew why Dorian wanted her to wear it, knew he wanted her nice and stretched for when he fucked her in the ass with his huge cock tonight.

Lubing up the plug, Lalita positioned herself so she was lying with her belly on the bed with her legs spread and her ass in the air. When the slippery tip touched her asshole, she instinctively clenched. Against her better judgment she bore down and started to slide it into her anus.

An uncomfortable feeling washed through her once it was fully imbedded, and she was surprised that there really was no pain. She would have thought she would be used to having big things shoved up her ass by now. Standing was an entirely different situation, though. The plug was pushed even farther inside of her when she stood her full weight, and she squeezed her eyes shut as she waited for the uncomfortable feeling to recede, which it didn't.

When she was ready per his specific instructions, she waited until that evening. Going all day with something shoved up her ass didn't seem like a fun time, but she went through the motions of her day. Just because it was Dorian's night didn't mean the others couldn't stroke her pussy, tease her breasts, or offer their cocks to her in wait for a blow job.

Even as she pleased everyone else, never once did she find her own release. She had a sneaking suspicion they had orders to make sure she suffered. By the time she finally saw Dorian, she would be so primed that just a flick of his finger over her clit and she would go off like an atomic bomb.

Despite the fact it was Dorian's night, she didn't see him all day. When she was back in her room after dinner, she waited with a rapidly beating heart for the moment when her bedroom door would open and he would come for her.

Time seemed to stand still until finally her door opened and in walked Dorian. He didn't speak, just ushered her to come to him. With knees feeling like Jell-O, Lalita made her way over to him and stood in front of him. No expression covered his face as he stared down at her.

"Follow me."

She didn't like his tone. It was cold and distant and void of any emotions. He turned and started walking down the hall without waiting to see if she'd follow. His long strides had her practically running to keep up with him. When he finally stopped, it was in front of a door that was all too familiar.

The bondage room came into full glory when he pushed the door open. The lights were already on and showcased everything with startling clarity. Heart pounding a mile a minute, she stepped into the room and heard the door close behind her.

"Go over to the bed and keep your back toward me."

Lalita did as he said, although with each passing moment she grew more and more uneasy. She didn't like this Dorian, didn't like how aloof and seemingly uncaring he was.

It felt like ages as she stood with her back to him, but then she felt a large hand land on her lower back and push her onto the bed. She was so surprised by the sudden movement that she fell forward and bounced off the mattress once.

Hands smoothed over her bare ass cheeks, and then her legs were nudged apart. Biting her lip was the only thing she could do to stop the sound that would have broke from her at the sudden motion of the plug shifting in her ass.

She couldn't see what was going on behind her, but she could hear the sound of a belt buckle being undone and a zipper being pulled down. The snaps that held the anal plug in place were next to go. It was clear he had a plan in mind because he didn't waste any time getting on with it.

Sheets bunched in her fists, she felt Dorian grip the anal plug and start to fuck her ass with it. It didn't hurt, but it also wasn't the most pleasant feeling. After a minute he pulled the plug out. She could only imagine what her ass looked like, all open and spread from the plug. Her pussy was wet, but she was so nervous her arousal was temporarily blinded.

"Do you know what I'm going to do to you tonight?"

It was instinct to turn and look at him, but as she turned to do just that a hard slap landed on one of her ass cheeks.

"I didn't give you permission to look at me. I asked you a simple question, so answer it."

Heart all the way in her throat, she knew Dorian was dominant and powerful, but never had she seen this side of him. It was intense. *He* was intense.

What was the point in beating around the bush? They both knew what he had planned, so she might as well just spit it out. "You plan on fucking me in the ass, Sir." The last part had been an afterthought, but she was glad she had remembered what a good little submissive ended her sentences with.

"You're absolutely right." He smoothed a hand down the crease of her ass and rimmed her hole with the digit. Her anus was lubed already, so when he pushed his thick finger into her, there was no resistance. He went with the motion of stretching his fingers out inside of her.

"I'm going to get right down to fucking this ass. I've been waiting to do so since you first arrived." The bed shifted as he settled between her spread thighs.

He was right. He didn't waste any time. She felt the tip of his cock press against the opening of her ass, and then he was pushing into her. There was a slight sting of pain as the thick crown pushed through the tight ring of muscle, but the plug had done a good job of opening her up, so he had little problem pushing into her the rest of the way.

Harsh breathing sounded behind her as he plowed her ass. "Tell me you want it harder and faster."

With each stroke, she was finding his momentum pushed her on the bed, which in turn had her clit rubbing on the sheets. Arousal peaking, she knew that if he kept this up she would finally be able to get off after being denied all day.

Without being able to hold in her words, Lalita moaned, "Fuck me harder, faster."

"I'm going to pound this ass so good that every time you sit down it'll be tender and you'll think about me."

"Oh God." His words did something wicked to her body. A sharp slap on her ass had her biting her bottom lip in pleasure.

"You are not allowed to speak, and you are not allowed to come." He slapped her ass cheeks so many times that they grew numb.

Situating her knees on the bed, she lifted her ass higher. She did want it harder and deeper. His balls slapped against her pussy and heightened her pleasure until she bit her lip so hard to try and hold off her climax she tasted blood.

Right when she was on the pinnacle of coming, Dorian pulled out of her with a groan. The sound of skin slapping against skin let her know he was jerking off, and then the feel of his hot spunk on her spread ass and pussy confirmed it.

This was misery, pure and simple. She needed to get off so bad she could taste it. She was flipped around suddenly. Legs flopped on each side, her pussy was wide open. Dorian knelt between her thighs, still-hard cock in hand, dark eyes trained on her cunt. She thought, for one small moment, that he might be merciful and give her what she needed, but she should have known that wasn't the case by the look on his face.

A droplet of cum was poised at the tip of his cock before falling and landing on her inner thigh.

"Get off the bed and go over there." He pointed to the X-shaped table. "Take the bra and garters off. You're not going to need them for what I have planned next."

She eyed the table and then him, knowing that whatever he had planned next might be a little too much for her to handle.

Chapter Fifteen

Everything that happened next seemed to go in slow motion. When Lalita was naked, Dorian pulled out a blindfold and secured it around her head. He then helped her onto the table, where she felt him restrain her hands and feet.

She sensed him move away from her and then heard the sound of running water. The table was shaped so that her legs were as wide as they could go without causing serious damage, which in turn meant both her pussy and asshole were available for penetration.

When she was situated how Dorian saw fit, silence filled the room. She anticipated what would happen next, maybe some whipping or electrical play, but when she heard a door open, she actually grew scared. She didn't think he would leave her alone in this position, but there was that fear of being helpless that had her skin started to bead with perspiration.

It wasn't until she heard the sound of numerous sets of feet entering the room and coming closer to her that Lalita realized she was in for one hell of a night. Apparently Dorian was in the mood to share, and she was the main course.

Hands from every direction started touching her body. With the blindfold around her head, her other senses seemed heightened. She could smell several different colognes, some wild and spicy, others earthy. Heavy breathing sounded all around her, some fast, some deep and hard.

Her hearing seemed more attuned as well, because she could hear a tiny whirling noise a moment before the table started to rise and tilt backward. Hands moved more demandingly on her body. Her nipples were tweaked until pain blossomed at the tips and the blood rushed to the surface. A warm mouth on her pussy is what she felt next, and it took everything inside of her not to cry out for more.

When a mouth latched onto each nipple and started licking and tugging at the turgid peaks, she wished she could thrust her chest deeper into their mouths. Tongues were on her breasts and pussy, and she couldn't stop the shaking that took control of her body.

Fingers spread her pussy lips apart while a tongue pumped in and out of her. It was too much at one time.

"Enough." Dorian's voice was like a bucket of cold water. It was so commanding that suddenly every mouth and hand that was on her moved away until she shivered from the lack of body heat.

Before she could contemplate what was next, a shaft slammed into her pussy with such force she couldn't hold back the cry that came from her. Deep, hard thrusts filled her, and before she knew it she was climaxing. Even if she could have stopped it, which was not likely, she didn't think she would have. It was hours upon hours of anticipation and teasing. It felt too damn good.

With her mouth open and the cry of rapture spilling from her tongue, someone thought it a good idea to shove a cock in there. As soon as she tasted that smooth, velvety skin over iron, she sucked like her life depended on it. It made it all that more exciting that she didn't know whose dick was in her mouth or who fucked her. It was excitement times ten, and she loved it.

Another cock ran along the other side of her cheek, and she instinctively let go of the shaft she sucked on and turned her head to engulf the other one. Her jaw ached from their thick erections, but it didn't matter. Another intense orgasm climbed to the surface.

The man fucking her gave a deep groan a second before he pulled out of her. Hot jets of liquid splashed along her belly for just a moment, and then another hard penis was pushed into her and fucking her madly.

Over and over they did this, switching off fucking her and making her suck their dicks until she was covered in their cum and exhausted from the multiple orgasms. If that wasn't enough, they turned the table so her ass was raised and presented. That hole was fucked numerous times, too, but between blacking out from the pleasure and crying out for more, Lalita didn't know what was up or down.

When she couldn't hold her head up any longer and the guys seemed to have had enough, she felt someone untie her hands and feet and take off the blindfold. She didn't bother opening her eyes as someone carried her to the bed and slipped in beside her. The sheets covered her next, and that was all she remembered before she blissfully let the darkness take her away.

* * * *

The next morning Lalita woke up sore and alone in not only the "dungeon" room but also the house. A note instructing her that a car would pick her up promptly at noon lay on the kitchen table when she finally made it downstairs. That note was a fucking kick in the gut. A white piece of paper that made her feel like a lowly piece of shit.

"They couldn't even say bye." *What the hell do you expect, you stupid girl.* In the end the only thing that mattered was seeing Lennon. Per their agreement, her money was already in her account. She had a lot of plans with that money, plans that would change her life as well as her son's.

She packed quickly and straightened up her room. No doubt the next girl would be staying there. With a little bit of time before the car showed up, Lalita went down the familiar hallway she had when she first arrived at the estate and stopped in front of the same picture she had looked at all those weeks ago.

The men looked like wax figurines, all stiff and unloving as they stared at the camera. She walked up and down some of the other hallways and even stopped out in the garden. She would really miss the garden. Hell, she would miss the whole estate.

A car horn honked, and she gave one last lingering look at the grounds before heading back inside to grab her things and leave this all behind her for good.

* * * *

As the weeks turned into months following her stay at the estate, Lalita found it easier to not think about Dorian or the other men. It had been hard to push the guys from her mind when she first came home, but being with her son helped to keep her mind clear. There were still times when she lay alone at night and close her eyes, picturing Dorian, Michael, Torryn, and even Aleck's hands on her body. Sometimes she even found herself tearing up thinking about him. She disgusted herself.

True to their word, the money had been in her account when she checked it the night she got home. Already she had done so much with it to benefit her and Lennon's lives. She had already found a nice little home he could grow up in, one with an actual backyard big enough for a swing set. The house may have been small, but they could call it home.

As she sat on the porch and watched Lennon play in the grass, she spread the newspaper out before her. The early afternoon sun heated her skin, and she closed her eyes and let it sink in. When she finally opened them and looked down at the paper, the lemonade that she had been about to swallow sprayed from her lips. Thankfully Lennon was too engrossed in his trucks to realize the mess she made, because how in the hell could she explain her actions to a five-year-old?

Staring back at her in black and white were Dorian and the other five men she had spent several months with. They all wore suits, their power so tangible that she could feel it even through the paper.

As she read the caption, her mouth went dry. They were known in the elite world as the "Powerful Six." She had known they were wealthy, had known they all held power somewhere, but she would have never guessed she had spent all that time fucking the McKinleys. Not only did that last name ring a bell to her, it was widely known throughout the country, throughout the world, in fact.

It now made even more sense why the contract had specified she was never to speak of this to anyone. She had just assumed it was standard text, but now she knew the specifics of it. If word got out that six McKinleys, ranging from lawyers to CEOs to a doctor, had paid a small fortune to sexually have a woman at their beck and call, their entire empire would crumble.

Stunned speechless by this, she continued to read. Apparently Torryn, Kane, and Zakary were brothers and owned the country's most prestigious law firm. Aleck, Michael, and Dorian were brothers and cousins to the other three.

When she first met Aleck, she would have never thought him to be one of the CEOs of the country's largest pharmaceutical companies because he came across as so laid-back. After they played in the "dungeon," it was clear he was commanding and held an inner self that spoke of a true leader.

She wasn't shocked at all to find out Dorian was a renowned surgeon. She remembered all too well how he had tended to her injury, and the times when his touch seemed so caring. She couldn't help but think back to the last night with him. It had been so clinical and non-emotional that even thinking about it now made her tear up.

Torryn was a renowned attorney, one of the best in the country. The paper called him a beast in the courtroom, a man that could clear anyone's name. Michael was also another CEO, one that was known as "The Bear" whenever his name was mentioned because of his gruff and dominating demeanor.

"What's wrong, Momma?"

Lennon's tiny voice broke through her thoughts, and she smiled at him. "Nothing, honey. Mommy's just thinking and being silly."

"Are you sad?"

How could she answer that honestly? Instead of telling her son the truth and having him ask her the numerous questions that were sure to follow, she just shook her head and pulled him into her arms.

"Go inside and change your shirt. Auntie Mary will be here in a little bit to take you and Megan to the birthday party." Lennon ran inside and slammed the door behind him. Lalita took one last look at the newspaper before folding it up and throwing it away.

The sound of Megan's voice right outside her front door an hour later caused Lennon to be in an uproar. Tiny giggles and talk of cake, presents, and ice cream filled their conversation. Lalita gave Mary a sympathetic look as she watched her best friend wrangle the two children into her car.

"You sure you don't want me to come with you?" Lalita grabbed the presents that had fallen and tucked them in the back of the vehicle.

"No. I've seen all the crap you still have yet to unpack."

"Does it look that bad?" Mary closed the door and turned to look at her.

"Yes, it does." Mary smiled. "We'll be back this evening."

As the car disappeared down the street, Lalita headed inside to first eat and then get up the courage to unpack the numerous boxes that still lined her house. Although Mary had questioned her about her stay at the estate, Lalita had left many details out. For one thing she hadn't divulged any of their names or what they had done, exactly. Lalita didn't want to speak about them and have her true feelings portrayed on her face, which she knew would be the case. Thankfully Mary had been content with what she had been told.

Chapter Sixteen

Lalita sliced fresh tomatoes and laid them beside the lettuce for her sandwich. She was procrastinating. She had cleaned the kitchen from top to bottom, both bathrooms, and the living room, but she had yet to unpack one single box.

The knife went through the tomatoes so easily and her mind was so preoccupied that when there was a loud bang on her front door, she jumped. Her surprise caused the knife to slip and slice right into her palm. Gasping and dropping the knife, she held her hand as blood started to seep out of the cut. Another loud bang on her front door caused her to jump into action instead of staring at the blood running down her forearm.

Grabbing a towel and haphazardly wrapping it around her hand, she went over to the front door, tripping over a box in the process. When she finally opened the door, her hand throbbed and her shin ached from the near fall, but all that pain disappeared when she stared at the four men on the other side.

They all wore dark suits and equally dark sunglasses. The car behind them reeked of money as it all but glistened in the driveway of her modest two-bedroom home.

The man closest to her removed the sunglasses. Eyes that had seemed so dark all those months ago looked lighter, almost warm. "Hi. Can we come in?"

Lalita was just too shocked to see Dorian, Michael, Torryn, and Aleck standing on her front porch that her throat closed, and no words made it past her lips. Dorian must have taken that as a refusal to his question because he dropped his head and sighed.

"I know we have no right just showing up like this, but please, will you let us in for just a short while? We just want to talk."

The sound of something dripping drew all of their attention. Blood slid down her arm and splashed on the ground. The pain she had felt before she had seen the four of them came back full force.

Dorian stepped through the doorway. Torryn, Michael, and Aleck followed. Dorian grabbed her arm and unwrapped the rag from her hand. "My God, Lalita. What happened?" He was all but pulling her into the kitchen and had her hand under the faucet before she even knew what was going on.

"Do you have a first-aid kit?"

She looked around and saw Torryn, Michael, and Aleck's worried expressions. She was too shocked to see the four of them in her home that she didn't answer right away.

"Lalita?"

Looking back at Dorian, she nodded and said, "Yes, in one of these boxes."

Dorian looked around at the chaos that made up her house. "I have my bag in my car. Sit down and keep pressure on the wound. I'll be right back." He wrapped the rag around her hand tight, gently pushed her down into one of the kitchen chairs, and headed out the door. The other three men didn't speak, just stared at the massacre that was becoming her kitchen. They did seem genuinely scared, though, as if the sight of blood was a little too much for them to handle.

Thankfully Dorian was back a moment later, and she didn't have to comfort Torryn, Michael, and Aleck, who seemed like they were about to pass out.

As she watched Dorian take out several items from the bag, memories of her time at the estate played through her mind. The four of them were actually in her home.

Even though nothing was being said at the moment, the fact that their presence was all around her comforted her. "Not to sound rude or unappreciative, but what are you guys doing here?" Dorian kept his head down, and when she looked at the other three, they shifted as if uncomfortable with her question. Dorian didn't respond until after he cleaned the cut and wrapped it in gauze. A pat on her bandaged hand was his cue that he was done.

The old wooden chair he sat in squeaked when he leaned back, and Lalita felt her face heat. Everything in her house was old, and they were not considered antiques. He stared at her, his dark eyes seeming lighter, less harsh in the afternoon light.

"I, *we*, meant to be there the day you left, but we couldn't bring ourselves to do it."

The letter that was left brought back feelings that she had slowly started to bury. Just seeing the four of them here in the flesh was painful in itself, but hearing him talk about their time at the estate was excruciating.

"I'm not really sure what you're getting at."

Torryn took a deep breath and stepped forward. "We shouldn't have let things get the way they did."

Her anger rose with ease passing moment. How dare they come to her home and lecture her on what they shouldn't have let get out of control. She may be a fool for feeling anything for them, but she was a human being, for fuck's sake. She opened her mouth to tell Torryn, to tell all of them, to get the hell out of her house, but Aleck lifted his hand to stop her as if he knew what was coming.

"Gauging the expression on your face, I can tell you've taken what Torryn said out of context." He reached across the table and encased her uninjured hand in his much bigger one.

Michael interjected. "What he meant to say is we shouldn't have hidden our feelings for you, Lalita."

Stunned speechless wasn't even the right term for how she felt at that moment.

Dorian cleared his throat and took her other hand in his. "I have been doing a lot of thinking since you left. I realized what an incredible ass I've been." He looked at his brothers. "We all were asses." He shook his dark head before continuing. "After you left, we sat down and laid it all bare. We each had feelings for you that had grown since the moment you stepped into our lives."

Torryn stepped forward and said, "We were just scared of what we felt for you. It isn't an excuse, we know that, but we wanted you to know."

With her mouth hanging open and her eyes probably looking like they were the size of saucers, Lalita probably looked like an idiot, but hearing each of them actually confess his feelings for her was a little surreal. Sure, she had hoped for this exact moment a million times, but when actually faced with it, she didn't know what to say or do.

She took a deep, steadying breath. "I'm not sure what to say. I can't forget what happened at the estate." Aleck and Dorian gave her hand a squeeze before letting it go.

"I can't blame you for wanting nothing to do with us. Not after the way we acted." Dorian grabbed his bag and stood. Torryn, Michael, and Aleck moved away from her and the four of them headed toward the front door. Lalita's heart started to pound something fierce.

Michael stopped and looked at her over his shoulder. "Anyway, we just had to tell you how sorry we are for the things that happened and the way we acted."

Torryn spoke next. "We do care for you. I love you, Lalita"

"I love you too, honey." Michael spoke, his voice hoarse and gravelly.

"As do I, sweetie. The way we met and the entire situation may not have been ideal, but I'm really thankful you came into my life." Aleck moved closer to her and kissed her gently on the cheek.

Torryn and Michael did the same before moving away so Dorian could take his place. He leaned down and kissed her on the forehead, and then he whispered, "I love you, too."

Lalita could do nothing but stare at them as they walked past her and out the front door. When the door closed behind them, she was left in a deafening silence, the only company being her thoughts. *Do something, you stupid fool.* The courage to rise from her seat burst inside of her like a freight train. She took off out the front door and toward Dorian, Michael, Aleck, and Torryn. They were already in the car and pulling away when she rushed out of the house. She did the only thing she could think of. She yelled as loud as she could, praying they heard her.

"Stop." In a smaller voice, she said, "Please, stop."

No doubt she sounded like a lunatic, but she didn't care, not when she saw the brake lights flare a brilliant red. Dorian got out of the car and then Torryn, Michael, and Aleck were next. The four of them walked toward her, and she did the only thing that seemed to fit that moment. She ran up to first Torryn, wrapped her arms around his waist, and laid her head on his chest. She did the same thing with Aleck, Michael, and finally Dorian.

"Lalita?" Voice sounding broken, Dorian pulled her back and stared down at her.

"I think you took my words out of context." She used the same line they did and couldn't help but smile. "What I meant was that my feelings for the four of you can't be forgotten, no matter how long I've been away." How could she say it in the simplest form without sounding like a total fool? She looked at each of them then, smiled, and just said it. "I love you, too. All four of you."

Epilogue

In the beginning of their relationship, Lalita, Dorian, Michael, Torryn, and Aleck thought it was best to take things slow. It wasn't because they didn't want to rush into things, hell, she had slept with all of them for several months.

Lennon took to them right away, which Lalita was thankful for, because even though she loved them, if her little man hadn't liked the four of them, it would have been a deal breaker.

Her four men seemed quite possessive of her, and Lalita would be lying if she didn't admit she loved it. There were times when all four would want to be intimate with her at the same time. Those times were extreme and made her breathless. Other times she would have alone time with each man. It was those times, when it was just two bodies pressed together, that she really felt the love between them.

Before Kane and Zakary found pretty little college girls to slake their appetites, they had been adamant on joining in on their "relationship," but Dorian, Michael, Aleck, and Torryn had made it clear that what they had went far beyond sex.

Eventually everyone had found their place in life, and Lalita couldn't be happier. Even a year and a half after her four men had showed up at her house, her feelings for them hadn't changed. In fact, they had just grown stronger. She still got butterflies in her belly every time she looked at them.

They were finally taking that next step in their lives and moving in together. Despite her protests, Dorian, Michael, Torryn, and Aleck insisted on getting a new place, one that would be new to them and they could raise Lennon in. That had been what had won her over.

The four of them cared about Lennon as if he was their own, and her little boy loved all of them the same. Although her son was much too young to fully understand the complex relationship she had with Dorian, Michael, Aleck, and Torryn, he was happy, and that was all that mattered.

It was on a warm, sunny Saturday that they looked at the house she fell in love with. It wasn't modest by any means, but it had a white picket fence around the property and a creek that ran the length of the house.

"Well, what do you think?" The five of them stood in the large living room that overlooked the acres of evergreens and blue spruces.

"It's perfect." She probably sounded like a child in a candy store. Hell, that's how she felt.

"Are you sure it's big enough?" She turned an incredulous look at Dorian.

"Are you kidding? It has eight bedrooms alone, easily enough room for all of us." It may not be what Dorian, Michael, Torryn, or Aleck were used to, not living in a mansion with a million different rooms, but it was cozy and perfect and just dreamy.

"So you really like it?" Aleck wrapped his arms around her waist and kissed the side of her neck.

Smiling at him, she let her head fall back against his chest. "I love it."

"That's a relief." Torryn walked past her but not before laying a soft kiss on her lips.

"Because we already bought it." Michael winked at her.

Lalita couldn't help the squeal that left her. "Oh my God, really?" She wrapped her arms around Michael and then did the same to the other three. "You are the four most wonderful men in the world, and I love you all so very much. I can't wait to show Lennon."

"The little man has already seen it, picked out his room already, too." Dorian smiled widely.

Narrowing her eyes up at him, she wasn't surprised. "So that's where you all went last weekend."

"Guilty." The four of them said it in unison.

"We had to get his opinion and make sure it was to his standards. We also wanted to make sure this was a good place to do this." Dorian stepped away from her and reached into his coat pocket. When she saw the black velvet box and saw him go down on one knee, her heart stopped.

She looked at Torryn, Michael, and Aleck, wondering what their reactions would be. They smiled at her and stepped beside Dorian.

Torryn spoke first. "Although we can't all marry you, we knew from the very beginning that we wanted you to be a McKinley."

Hand over mouth so he didn't see how open it was, Lalita stared with blurry eyes at the four of them. Dorian stared up at her and presented the most beautiful ring she had ever seen.

"Lalita Grace Marshall, will you do me the honor of being my wife?"

"Only technically, that is." Aleck winked at her when she glanced at him.

"We all want to think of you as our wife even though Dorian will legally be your husband." Michael leaned in and ran his hand down her cheek.

Tears flowed freely down her cheeks as she looked back down at Dorian. When she didn't say anything right away, she saw a worried look cross his face.

"Oh God."

He got back to his feet and cleared his throat. "Is that a yes?"

Throwing herself into his arms, she squeezed him as tight as she could. The tears refused to stop, but she could care less. "Yes, yes, and yes."

He wrapped his arms around her tighter. "That's good, because me and Lennon had a bet that you would faint before you gave me an answer. Looks like I won."

"You made a bet with my son?" The chuckle that came from her sounded watery and hoarse from her crying. "So what did you win?"

"His permission to marry you." Aleck, Michael, and Torryn cleared their throats, and she and Dorian looked over at them. "Well, he said he wouldn't mind having Torryn, Michael, and Aleck around, too."

"And if you would have lost?"

"We would have had to buy him a pony, which we are probably going to have to do anyway, because we don't think he'll let us out of it."

Lalita couldn't help but laugh. "No, he probably won't." Her heart swelled with love and happiness. There was nothing greater that she could have asked for than her son and the men that stood before her. She loved all of them more than life itself.

THE END

HTTP://WWW.JENIKASNOW.COM

ABOUT THE AUTHOR

Jenika is just your average woman. She lives in the too-hot northeast with her husband and their young daughter. Thankfully, he shares her unusual sense of humor and naughty nature, so finding material for her stories isn't a problem.

Along with taking care of their daughter, they have to keep an eye on Milo and Otis, their spunky cats. Jenika writes erotic paranormal, contemporary, BDSM, and sci-fi romances.

Jenika started writing at a very young age. Her first story consisted of a young girl who traveled to an exotic island and found a magical doll. That story has long since disappeared, but her passion for writing has stayed strong.

Jenika loves to hear from readers and encourages them to contact her and give their feedback.

Also by Jenika Snow

Siren Classic: Dimi of the Seven Moons 1: *Deliciously Wicked*
Siren Classic: Dimi of the Seven Moons 2: *Temptation Unveiled*
Siren Classic: Blood Breed: *The Chosen: A Tale of the Blood Breed*
Siren Classic: *Blush: A Story of Dominance and Submission*
Ménage Amour: *Bittersweet: A Story of Dominance and Submission*
Siren Classic: Alpha One Assassins: *The Assassin*
Ménage Amour: *Lilly's Surrender*

Available at
BOOKSTRAND.COM

Siren Publishing, Inc.
www.SirenPublishing.com

Lightning Source UK Ltd.
Milton Keynes UK
UKOW03f1402030913

216451UK00021B/1923/P